Message in a Bottle

Message in a Bottle

Jenny Koralek

Illustrated by Kate Fitzsimon

Lutterworth Press
Cambridge

To Joanna Haggarty

and to Patrick Hardy
in praise of friendship

Lutterworth Press
7 All Saints' Passage
Cambridge CB2 3LS

British Library Cataloguing in Publication Data
Koralek, Jenny
  Message in a bottle
  I. Title II. Fitzsimon, Kate
  823′.914[J] PZ7

ISBN 0-7188-2655-8

First published 1987 by Lutterworth Press

Printed in Great Britain by St. Edmundsbury Press

CONTENTS

1 . Map's End Sleeping

The grandfather clock struck five as Jane Finch crossed the cool, dark hall. The solid front door lay wide open behind her. The smell of honeysuckle had blown in with her, and great rays of dusty sunshine warmed her bare legs.

"Not long now," she whispered. "He said to be ready at half past five. *And* no school tomorrow. No more school for six whole weeks!" She felt like hugging herself and the grandfather clock or dancing a wild jig. The teacup, which she was carrying upstairs to her mother, began to wobble in its saucer, no longer neatly centred.

"I'm going in half an hour," Jane called back to her father who was stretched out on the lawn reading the paper. "Remember? I'm going to the beach with Mr Eliot."

"Right you are." Mr Finch yawned and beamed as the harmless small white clouds fluffed few and far between across the July sky. Jane's parents were farmers. Busy and brisk all week with their acres and acres of crops, their large gentle cows and huge flocks of sheep, on Sunday afternoons they always put their feet up in favourite places and Jane always brought them tea.

"Oh dear," said Jane, in the doorway of her mother's room. "I've spilt it again."

"You always sound so surprised," said her mother, curled up sleepily in the old armchair by the window. "Why don't you try using a tray?"

"You say that every week," Jane said.

"And what a waste of breath!" laughed her mother. "Thanks all the same. I'm dying for my cuppa . . ."

Jane leaned against the tall window and looked out at her world asleep in the Sunday lull. There lay the farm. All its sights, sounds and smells had long since seeped deep into her: the sickly-sweet warm milk, the fragrant hay, wool tufts on barbed wire, dry sheep droppings, flat cow-pats; the blistery-looking ice on frozen tractor puddles, prickly straw and sneezy chaff; screeching machines, humming machines, bleats, barks, cockerel cacophony and mud, mud, mud. But not today. Today the earth baked and crumbled. It hadn't rained for weeks. The green alders and the white willows shimmered in the water-meadow, the one place that stayed boggy and puddly all year round. Jane's boat, *The Ark*, lay docked, strangely high and dry on the bank of the quiet brown river; and beyond loomed the dark downs, the railway below them, the sea lurking behind them. Jane's eyes returned to her strange boat. Found for her when her brother, Toby, went off to Australia to try his hand at shearing sheep, Jane knew her parents had hoped she'd have hours of fun in it with friends. It even had its own little house amidships, sturdy and well-furnished, but Jane wasn't much of a housewife and her friends had lately all gone pony mad. So there it lay, no longer afloat, like the ark abandoned after the flood. It always made her uneasy, like a heavy question she didn't want to hear or answer. What's the use of a boat out of water? Well, she wasn't going to think about it now, not on the first day of the holidays.

She stared down at the tiny village of Map's End. It really was at the end of the map. The only road ended in the river. "You live in the sticks." That's what that cocky new girl, Mary, had said. Mary Selby, who'd only been at school one term and already taken Susan Barnes away from her.

Map's End. It wasn't even a proper village. There was no shop, no post office, no pub; just the farm, two cottages snuggled by the church with its crooked weathercock – and New House, old long before Queen Victoria lay in her cradle. If New House was new, Jane often wondered, then what on earth was old?

"Do you know," Jane said, turning to her mother, "Mr Eliot and me are the only ones who were actually born here, born at Map's End? Not you, not Dad, not the Gurneys, not even Toby . . ."

"You were born in this very room," said Mrs Finch. "On the coldest day since the freeze of '47. Mr Eliot told me that."

"Three feet of snow outside the front door . . ." Jane joined in. She'd heard it all before, but still loved to hear.

"Couldn't possibly have got to the hospital in time," they finished together.

"You wanted me born here, didn't you?"

"Yes," her mother smiled.

"Out riding just before I came, weren't you?"

"Yes," admitted her mother.

Jane sat down on the floor at Mrs Finch's feet. "You know," she said, fiddling with the fringe on the armchair. "I don't miss Toby as much as I did."

"Good," said Mrs Finch. "It would be awful if you were still mooching and moping about as much as you did when he first went away."

"Do you remember when I tried digging that tunnel to Australia on the beach?"

"I certainly do – like a puppy frantically looking for a bone."

"I got so cross! *And* I never even got to Bognor and you can see that from the beach!"

"The other side of the world," her mother sighed.

"Do you miss Toby *very* much?"

"Of course, but he's grown up now. High time he left home and got on with his own life."

"Maybe one day you and Dad can go out and see him!"

"Maybe."

"Maybe he's saving the fare up right now to come and see us."

"Maybe." Mrs Finch patted Jane's arm. "You mustn't be late for Mr Eliot."

"Galloping snails!" Jane leapt to her feet. "I must scoot, but I'll be back in time to feed the ponies. Promise!"

"*Feed!*" Mrs Finch laughed. "Those terrible fatties. What Tweedledum and Tweedledee need more than anything is exercise. Come riding with me tomorrow? It would halve the time if we took one fatty each."

"All right," Jane said hesitantly. Then spun away to the door. "But only if you let me slide down the banisters," she called from the top of the stairs. "Haven't done it for ages . . . S-e-e y-o-u . . ." Her voice faded, word by whizzing word.

"Horse-lover of the year!" Mrs Finch called after her. "Have fun!"

Jane was lucky to have Mr Eliot. She was very young and he was very old but they found each other excellent company. He lived by himself in New House; soon after Toby had gone, Mr Eliot had invited Jane to tea and a game of Beggar-my-neighbour. Before long Jane had learned to weave her way in and out of the old man's quiet life in a way that suited them both. And now, nearly every day, even if it was only for a minute, Jane would dash through the gate in the orchard wall to visit him. If it was the wrong moment he always said so straight out and she would dash off again. "Lucky it's a gate and not a hedge," Mrs Gurney often said. She packed eggs at the farm and cleaned New House whenever Mr Eliot would let her, which wasn't nearly as often as she would have liked. "Lucky it isn't a hedge," Mrs Gurney would say, "or by now you'd have an almighty hole in it."

On rainy days they might play Monopoly in Mr Eliot's den, or tell each other terrifying ghost stories, or Jane would tinker with the miniature garden he had let her set up on a wobbly card-table, while he puffed on his pipe and read the paper. When there was snow on the ground they would fling open the door of the kitchen range, draw up chairs and toast marshmallows on a long, queer old three-pronged fork. Then – and only then – Mr Eliot allowed Jane to warm her toes on top of the range. She had to watch her socks very carefully; if they singed there was an awful smell which clashed with the marshmallows so that suddenly she didn't feel greedy for them any more.

Mr Eliot showed her the hidden swing in the garden; told her she could go there at any time. And then, one day, when she was off school getting over chicken-pox, Mr Eliot showed her the dusty, dim-lit attic. He pointed out the doll's house, a model of New House which Jane found rather boring. He lifted the creaky lid of a chest full of old-fashioned clothes – bright and tender silks and velvets, tickly ostrich feathers and fans. "You could dress up in these," he said.

"Mmm," said Jane.

"Or there's old Stargazy." Mr Eliot patted the enormous rocking-horse. "No running after him with sugar lumps, no fiddling with girths, *no rubbing down*! Think of that Jane, think of that!" No one who lived at Map's End could help knowing that Jane Finch was not a horsey girl.

Jane looked at the rocking-horse's proud snarling head and grinned. "I quite fancy a gallop on him," she said. "He can look as fierce as he likes but he's never going to topple me into a ditch . . ."

"Good lord!" cried Mr Eliot who was peering about in the gloom. "There are the dear old dogs."

"Dogs?" cried Jane. "Up here?"

"Silly," said Mr Eliot "China. There, do you see 'em? Spaniels. Large, Middling and Small. That's what we called them, me and my young sister. Hollow, you know." He picked up Large gently and turned him over. "See? They've each got a hole in the base. We used to hide things in them."

"What sort of things?"

"Oh, toffees and fossils and little notes to each other, saying 'Keep out you fat pig'."

" 'Keep out you fat pig'?" Jane laughed.

" 'Hands off my toffees' – that sort of thing," said Mr Eliot.

Jane stared at the dogs. Large's long ears drooped in a dignified way. White and lofty from top to toe, he stared, deadpan and bored, into some far distance. Middling looked much the same, but in a middling way – not quite so haughty, not quite so deadpan, because his nose was painted black, which made him look rather absurd and likeable.

Where the other two sat up straight, Small lay on his side. Thin strokes of gold outlined his floppy ears, his coat and his feathery tail, which almost wagged. His eager face was expectant, friendly. He looked as if he might come to life at any minute and beg to go out at once for a long walk.

8

"You can come up here any time you like. Play with anything you like," the old man had said.

"Can I?" said Jane. "Can I really?"

"Certainly, but don't expect me to join you. Those stairs seem to have got steeper with the years."

So little by little Jane had taken to creeping up to the attic. She rode the large, dappled rocking-horse without fear, and inside Large she hid a wren's egg wrapped in curly rust-gold pheasants' feathers. Later she added some small sea-shells and Dumpy, the minute wooden doll Toby had given her long long ago for good luck on her first day at school. Inside Middling she kept fruit gums and chocolate buttons. She never hid anything inside Small. He looked as if he couldn't keep secrets like the other two. Jane would sit on the old chest sucking sweets, staring and staring at Small, wishing he would come to life, or wishing Toby was still at home so she could leave notes in Large, saying *Keep out fat pig* or *I have spat on all these sweets.*

Mr Eliot and Jane always began her holidays with a walk. And on this first Sunday of the great summer holidays they were going to the beach. Jane called it the best walk.

Mr Eliot said he was too old now to get up on the downs, "or down the ups," so they often walked in the woods, or along the river bank. Jane loved the woods round Map's End, and the faithful river.

But the beach was different. It made her feel strange. It made her feel small, even though she could see forever there and stretch to a fathom.

The salt air made her breathe more deeply, tingled in her. And the sea, which changed all the time, excited her: choppy or smooth, blue or grey, or green with little white horses. Or like a mill-pond with boats becalmed in empty emptiness. Sighing, raging, tide in or tide out, raucous gulls or silent proud geese, it was not map's end there. It was map's beginning.

She had been longing all day for it to be half past five, but now, once she'd hurried through the garden wall, once she'd escaped the threat of having to go riding, Jane found her feet slowing down. She came to a standstill. It was so quiet. Was it a spell? No, thought Jane. It's not a spell. It's me. *I*'ve gone quiet. Like when I see a rainbow fading, or one fat raindrop just as it plops off a leaf. If I saw a unicorn now I wouldn't budge an inch.

"Lovely afternoon isn't it, Jane? Ever so still. You'd hear a leaf drop, if leaves were dropping."

Jane nearly jumped out of her skin. There was Mrs Gurney, peering at her over her garden wall. "Quiet before the storm, I'd say," she went on. "Only there's barely a cloud in the sky. Mind you, there's storms and storms I always say . . ."

"Yes," said Jane out loud, but 'old gas bag' to herself.

"I'm waiting for my Jean," said Mrs Gurney, leaning ever more cosily on her moss-topped wall. "She's dropping Pippa and Alice off so's she and Steve can get away on their own for a bit."

"Oh good," said Jane stiffly. She could feel the magic slithering away like a frightened snake back into some deep hole.

"Haven't had a holiday since little Alice was born."

"Poor things," Jane said coldly.

"Hope this weather holds. They're off to Jersey . . ."

"That's nice," Jane said dully. And then heard herself and was ashamed. Mrs Gurney sounded so pleased for her children, so happy. She was a busybody, but a kind busybody, watching over Map's End, the sky above it, the land it lay upon.

"It'll be a lot of extra work for you," Jane said, "having those little ones."

"I don't mind that," smiled Mrs Gurney. "They'll be company for me, and no trouble to my old man. He's always out a lot at this time of year – up on them blessed downs with that dog of his, looking for his precious orchids."

"Still hoping to find a new one?" asked Jane.

Mrs Gurney nodded. "Still, it keeps him out of the pub . . ."

Mr Eliot's car started up in the driveway of New House. Mrs Gurney's ears pricked up, her eyes brightened. "Off to the beach are you, then?"

"Yes, and I mustn't keep him waiting." Jane's feet came to life. She waved and dashed for the corner.

"Nosy old parker," she yelled freely into the ferocious revving noises of Mr Eliot's ancient car. "Oh drat! I've forgotten my shell bag."

2 . The Sea

Jane hurtled across the clattery shingle, well ahead of Mr Eliot. It was always like that on their walks: Jane out in front, Mr Eliot steadily bringing up the rear. It was for him, perhaps, rather like taking a puppy for a walk, only he tossed questions instead of sticks. "Cygnets still about?" he'd ask from the river bank. "Good year for holly berries?" on the path arched with oak and ash, entwined with old man's beard. Jane didn't always hurtle. For cygnets she crept, but she was always out in front, skinny, gawky, happy to dash back with some answers whispered, some shouted on the run.

When she got to the last singing stone at the very edge of the bumped-up shingle, Jane bent down to undo her sandals. "I've forgotten my shell bag," she called over her shoulder.

"Never mind," said Mr Eliot. "I've got pockets." He leaned against the breakwater, watching her little ritual. Then he turned to the sky; noted the small clouds, the windlessness, followed the path of a mob of rackety gulls. His bright eyes ranged over the waters, keen, careful, like a sailor at the wheel.

Jane watched her toes sink into the dark sand.

There was always just time to feel each one go down in a separate grainy squelch. She looked up. Mr Eliot seemed suddenly very far away from her. She ran to him and slipped her hand into his. "Come on," she urged, "come on, let's go to the rock pools and look for yellow shells."

"Yes," Mr Eliot agreed. "Let's walk a bit. It's good for these stiff old legs." He breathed deeply. "Ahhhh! The sea air, the briny . . ."

"You always say that," Jane smiled. She tried hard to slow her lanky legs to Mr Eliot's frail but steadfast tread.

"I know," laughed Mr Eliot.

"And 'smell of the country' every single time you go past a muck heap."

"Sorry I'm so predictable."

"So *what*?"

"Sorry you always know what I'm going to say."

"*I* don't mind," said Jane. "Think how horrid it would be if you went into your bedroom and found all the furniture changed round, or *new* . . ."

"True," agreed the old man.

They headed for the distant rock pools. The beach was emptying fast. Car doors slammed, dogs barked and children bickered. But in the sheltering white dunes a few families still lay stretched out with tea and transistors, unwilling to leave the warm sand, on holiday from clocks, lead pollution and flight paths over their back gardens.

"What a lot of people there are today," moaned Jane.

"Don't exaggerate," reproved Mr Eliot.

"Practically got the place to ourselves as usual. Trouble is, we're spoiled living down here all the time. Tend to forget, y'know, a lot of people wait all year for their two weeks by the sea."

"I know," said Jane, knowing that she didn't, not really.

Mr Eliot stopped and pulled a large handkerchief from his pocket, blew his nose and grunted. He always did that if he beat Jane at Monopoly, as if to say "that's that then".

"Looking forward to *your* holidays, eh Jane?" the old man asked. "Got any plans? Going to get up to a few capers with that nice girl Susan? Susan Whatsername?"

"Barnes," said Jane. "I don't think she'll be coming to stay this time."

"Oh dear," said Mr Eliot. "Whyever not?"

"I quarrelled with her," sighed Jane. "There's this beastly girl Mary – Mary Selby – she only came at the beginning of last term. It's very peculiar, you know, not to start at a new school at the proper time – and she's ganged up with Susan."

"Oh dear," said Mr Eliot. "Perhaps she's shy and feels out of it having come so late . . ."

"Perhaps," Jane said crisply. "Mary Selby and Susan go to all the gymkhanas together. Susan hardly ever used to go to any. And then they tried to make me join the Pony Club. I'm the only girl in the class, you see, who doesn't belong . . ."

"You sound proud of that," put in Mr Eliot.

Jane tossed her head. "I can't help it," she said, "I'm just not a horse-lover, that's all."

"Sure?" asked Mr Eliot.

"Quite sure," said Jane. "Oh look! There's a yellow shell." She darted away to the frothy edge of the shore where the last wave had worn itself out. "Oh no," she called back. "It's only a bit of plastic." She stood still and brooded on the garish yellow piece of nothing; then looked out to sea, empty today – empty of ships, wind-surfers, drift-wood.

"Want to paddle?" called Mr Eliot. "Cool off?" Jane turned towards him, her hands on her hips.

"No," she said crossly.

Mr Eliot joined her at the water-line, not bother-ing that his shoes were getting wet. He knew Jane felt big in her own woods and fields but small at the beach. "You look like Rumpelstiltskin," he said. "If you stamp your foot now you will most certainly end up in Australia."

"It's not funny," said Jane. She turned back to the sea again. Mr Eliot prodded the sand with his stick. "No luck, eh? Nothing doing here. Never mind, perhaps we'll find some further on . . . usually do . . . Look! We're nearly at the rock pools."

"It's not the *shells*," snapped Jane. "*Any*body can pick up shells."

"I know," soothed Mr Eliot. "I know, dear Jane. What is it then? What do you want?"

Jane rounded on him, her brown eyes tearless and fierce. "Something for me, specially. Just for me."

"Not somebody else's old boot?" asked Mr Eliot,

16

trying to fit Jane's sudden longing into the patch-work of her moods.

"Exactly not. Not shells, not an old boot, not an empty Coke bottle . . . That's it though! That's it! That's what I want!" She stared again at the very empty sea. "A bottle! I want a bottle to come bobbing straight towards me – with a message in it, a message only I can understand."

"I found one once," confessed Mr Eliot.

"Did you?" asked Jane enviously. "Did you really? What did it say? What did it say?"

Mr Eliot laughed. "Have one on me."

"Have one what?"

"A drink. People say that in pubs when they intend to pay for your drink.'

"Oh," said Jane, disappointed. "Well, did you? Have one, I mean?"

"As a matter of fact I had two. One for me and one for him, whoever he was. In the Pig and Whistle on my way home that same evening."

"Huh!" snorted Jane. "That's not my idea of a message in a bottle at all. It didn't tell you anything."

"It was a greeting," said Mr Eliot mildly. "From one fellow to another fellow. There's a lot to be said for greetings, I've always found. Why, what sort of message would you want in your bottle? Magic recipes? How to find friends at school? How to turn into a horse-lover overnight?"

"Don't laugh at me," Jane begged. "Please don't laugh at me."

"I'm not," protested Mr Eliot. "A friend doesn't laugh at; he laughs with."

"We-ell," admitted Jane. "I do wish I had more friends, and I do wish – for Mum's sake really – that I was a horse-lover. But it's not just that. Ohhh!" she wailed. "I don't understand anything."

"Don't exaggerate," said Mr Eliot. He patted her arm. "Count to ten and try again." Jane dabbled her toes for a long moment in the lazy, lapping water. She was much calmer when she spoke again, clear now about her wish, able now to look straight at Mr Eliot, old friend, the grandfather she had never known.

"When I come down here," Jane said quietly, "I always feel how big the world is and then I want to understand" – she couldn't help flinging her arms wide – "everything."

"Tall order," said Mr Eliot. "Why should you? Do you have rights?" He pointed with his stick to the sands, to the water. "I doubt they understand. They are what they are." He tapped gently at some mussels clinging to a rock. "Sometimes they make pearls," he murmured, "and sometimes they don't."

"But I'm not a shell," Jane insisted. "I'm a *person*. What about me?"

Mr Eliot settled himself against the rock and looked up at Jane with stern, kind eyes. "Ah," he breathed. "You. And you want your answers crammed into a bottle. Join in, dear Jane. Join in. That's the message, don't you see? That's the first commandment. I'm tired, my dear. Do you mind if I sit here while you pick up a few of those shells? D'you see them?" He pointed to a little patch not far away. "Stroke of luck, wouldn't you say? Almost washed up at our feet. After all, that's what we came looking for." He fished out his handkerchief again, blew his nose, closed his eyes and dozed in the bone-warming sun.

Jane crouched over the shells, dropping the perfect spirals into her palm, spangled with sand. "Stone the crows," she muttered. "Stone the flaming crows." The growly words, stolen from Mr Gurney, rumbled out to sea. She turned a shell over, stared at its curly dark opening. "I *do* join in. I go to school, don't I? I help wash up. I shut gates for Dad and feed Mum's precious fatties. Won't that do?"

She picked up the biggest shell and put it to her ear. It fitted neatly. The whole sea was in there, alive and roaring for her. And then the sea did another thing for Jane. It tossed a starfish at her feet. Its fingers pointed all ways, like the pattern a Catherine wheel makes when it just begins to spin. Jane stared at it with joy. She was tempted to pick it up and carry it home to put in the pond of her miniature garden. But then it would die. "I mustn't take you out of your world," she whispered. Even as she spoke the sea sucked the starfish back to itself. And Jane began to turn splashy cartwheels in the shallow water. Mr Eliot opened half an eye, smiled and eased his back into a smoother hollow.

3 . A Shock at Supper

Mr Eliot dropped Jane off at the farm gate, his wave, as usual, almost a salute.

She never saw him again.

The next evening the phone rang in the middle of supper.

Mr Finch swore and went to answer it.

"Why do people always ring at mealtimes?" Mrs Finch sighed. "His potatoes'll get cold." But Mr Finch was back very soon. Jane had a forkful of lettuce halfway to her mouth, but she put it down again. Her father was not sitting down. He was gripping the back of his chair, leaning forward a little, protective, serious.

"What is it, Jim? Who was it?" Mrs Finch was anxious.

"Old Sam Eliot died . . . half an hour ago. That was Dr Holmes . . . thought we'd like to know." Mr Finch spoke gruffly. His chair scraped with a nasty shriek on the stone floor as he sat down, picked up his knife and fork, put them down again.

"Dear old Sam," said Mrs Finch. "As he said himself at Easter, he'd had a good innings."

"It was very sudden, apparently," said Mr Finch. "Been complaining of feeling tired for the last

20

couple of days. Went swiftly and peacefully . . ."
Jane stared down at her plate – her favourite
summer supper: cold ham, cold beef, buttery,
minty new potatoes and salad splodged over with
lots of mayonnaise. She did not want to look at her
parents and she knew they did not want to look at
her.

"Dear Sam," said Mrs Finch again. "Of course,
he'd been living on borrowed time with his dicey
old ticker."

Mr Finch started cutting up his meat. Mrs Finch
crunched a radish.

Tears began to boil from Jane's eyes. She pushed
her plate away, knocking over a glass of water.

"How can you?" she shouted. "How can you sit
there *eating* when he's dead? It's my fault. It's my
fault. I must have made him tired at the beach."
She jumped up, rushed out of the room and
stumbled her way to the garden. *Good innings,
borrowed time, dicey old ticker*. The baffling words
buzzed round Jane's head. She flung her arms
round the trunk of the mulberry tree and began
to sob huge sobs that hurt the middle of her
stomach like a bad bruise. Suddenly her mother
was there, her father too. He pulled her firmly
from the hard tree; Jane buried herself in the
softness of her mother's body, her eyes shut tight.

"Jane, Jane," murmured her father. "Calm
down."

"I can't," she sobbed. "Not yet."

"Do you want to be by yourself?" asked her
mother.

"No," sobbed Jane, clinging closer. "No. Stay here . . . wait . . . just wait!"

"Of course we'll wait," said her father.

Very slowly, very unevenly, Jane's sobs juddered into hiccups and sniffs. Mr Finch passed her a handkerchief and she mopped at her face, blew her nose.

"Smells of oil. Smells horrible," she said.

"Tractor engine," smiled her father.

"What's a dicey ticker?"

"Oh Jane," sighed Mrs Finch. "That was just my very silly way of saying he had a bad heart."

"What's a good innings?"

"He meant he'd had a good long life."

"He knew he was going to die soon," added Mr Finch.

"Well, why didn't he tell me?" Jane was angry again.

"I expect he didn't want you to be sad . . . to spoil your times together," said her mother.

"Ye-es," Jane admitted. "He's . . . he was . . . like that. But I let him get tired. We walked too far. It was m-m-my fault."

"Drop it, Jane," said her father quite fiercely. "It was not your fault. You couldn't add to or lessen that kind of tiredness." The words were like a slap.

"Jim," protested Mrs Finch.

But Jane did not wince. "I'm ex-ex-aggerating, aren't I?"

"Yes," agreed her father. "I think you probably are."

"That's what he would have said." She almost

smiled at her father. He ruffled her hair.

"Come on, both of you now," urged Mrs Finch. "Come in and finish your supper."

"No," said Jane. "Not yet. I don't want to come in just yet. Now I do want to be by myself for a bit." She turned her smudgy face towards her parents. "See? I'm not crying any more."

"All right," said her mother, "but don't stay too long."

Jane slithered to the ground, her back against the tree, all words washed out. The sun was going down. A heron flapped up over the river and settled again. Cows in the near field munched and moved through lush grass. And the mulberry leaves rustled as if a breath was passing through them.

When Mrs Finch came back a little later with a bowl of raspberries and cream, Jane was fast asleep.

4 . Through a Glass Darkly

During the days before Mr Eliot's funeral her mother kept Jane busy. Obediently she cleaned out all the kitchen cupboards, attacking sticky jam-jar circles and the dribbles on the ketchup bottle; she washed up after each meal, scrubbed fiercely at pots and pans, helped Mrs Gurney pack eggs.

Stonily, she stood at the back of the church during the funeral service. She heard strong words in fragments, some mysterious, clouding her in puzzlement, some comforting: *this our brother, of the earth earthy, though he die, yet shall he live, glory of the sun, glory of the moon, through a glass darkly, faith, hope, love.* She stumbled after the many mourners, watching the coffin held high by six strong men. Some of them had been crying. One of them was her own father. The sheep grazing in the church-yard scattered, blundering over old grassy mounds, knocking into mossy headstones: marble, granite, angels, crosses.

Jane watched the coffin laid in the deep grave beneath the farthest yew below the walls of New House. Then she went away. She went to the swing. Across Mr Eliot's empty garden to the dark holm-oak which hid from everyone but her the

long-forgotten damp green slat, dangling on crooked ropes. Now only Jane knew the safe path through the nettles into the heart of the giant thicket. She flopped back on the swing so her straight brown hair touched the dusty ground. Shimmers of sunlight dazzled through chinks in the narrow leaves and made her eyes water. She gave the swing a tetchy little shove.

Jane was angry with Mr Eliot. He hadn't even said goodbye. Where had he gone? She must know. Now. She shoved the swing a little harder, impatient again for some neat, clear message, some answer. But there was a great silence behind the hot buzz of summer. She jabbed her sandals into the swirls of dry earth, stabbing out angry zig-zags. And stoniness settled on her.

"You know," said Mrs Finch at breakfast next day, "I've been worrying about Mrs Gurney and the eggs. Somehow I don't think collecting and packing eggs goes with Alice and Pippa, do you?"

"Mu–um," Jane sighed. "If you want me to do the eggs for a bit why don't you just ask me straight out?"

"Well, it would be a great help, darling. Mrs Gurney really has her hands full. I'm sure she'd be only too glad of the break. And then I can get on with the jam. All those redcurrants. Never seen such a year for soft fruit . . . and Tweedledum and Tweedledee always needing exercise . . ."

"If you are going to do the eggs, Jane," Mr Finch put in, "one of those darned hens has gone walkabout. Broody, silly thing. Quite the wrong time of year for hatching chicks."

"You don't miss much, Dad," said Jane. "How on earth do you know there's a hen missing out of all that lot?"

"There is only one black hen, did you never notice?" her father asked. "Haven't seen her for several days now. You could try looking for her. I mean, there's free range and free range. I've fixed the gap in the wire where she must have got out. Don't want the others going and getting any ideas."

Jane leaned over the table and put her hand on her mother's. "If you li-ike . . . I'll help you with TD and TD as well."

"That is sweet of you, Jane," smiled her mother, "but see how you get on with the eggs first. That'll keep you busy, specially if you have to go on a hen-hunt as well."

"Don't overdo it, Jane," laughed her father, "or next thing you'll be saying your holidays were nothing but slave labour."

"No," protested Jane. "I'm in the mood."

"I know it's rather boring for you here on your own," said Mrs Finch. "Sure you wouldn't like to ask Susan to stay?"

"No," said Jane. "And anyway she's much too busy these days with Mary Selby and the Pony Club."

Her parents struggled bravely not to exchange glances.

"I don't feel like people. I'd rather be doing things. Maybe I could even start scraping *The Ark*'s bottom."

"Hull," said Mr Finch.

"Hull," Jane corrected herself.

"What has come over you?" Mrs Finch couldn't help saying.

"Nothing. Oh, I don't know. It must be the weather. Makes you want to be out of doors. I'll go and get the eggs now."

5 . Trespassing

Jane filled the baskets carefully – ten, twelve, seventeen, nineteen, twenty, twenty-one. Not so many as some days. She carried them back to the dairy, then stood and looked about her. The air was still, the sun already very warm. A heat-haze hung over the water-meadow. By noon any shadow would be welcome, the call of any water hard to resist. "Better get after that broody hen straight away," Jane decided. "Now, if I was a daft hen and lived on this farm, where would I go to lay my eggs? Mm . . . somewhere nice and quiet and cool . . . I know! I know where I'd go! Down to the river. That's where I'd go. Down in the reeds and the rushes – to the ducks' nests, the swans' nests. Like the ugly duckling back to front!"

She crossed the lane and climbed into the water-meadow, puddle-hopping from turf to turf. Sure she was on the right track, the only track, she hurried past *The Ark*'s looming hulk. The fun of the hunt reminded her of Easter. She could hardly wait to get her hands round those eggs.

"Excuse me." The voice was polite and came from the air. "Have you lost a black hen by any chance?" Jane jumped as if she'd been spattered with air pellets. "I'm afraid you're trespassing," the voice went on. "Because of the hen ... I suppose ... if it's yours ..."

Jane spun round. Fright, then rage, like greedy ogres, gobbled up her fun, her delight in the bright, fresh day. For there, standing on the deck of her boat, her very own boat, on her own land, was a completely strange boy, peering at her, either because the sun was in his eyes, or because he wasn't wearing glasses when he should have been – or both.

"Get down," Jane yelled, hands on hips. "Get down at once. Get off my boat."

"*Your* boat?" The boy even had the nerve to sound disappointed, as if he thought somehow it might belong to him. All the same, he backed away from the rail quite smartly. "Okay. Sorry. I'll come down at once." And he stumbled down the ladder into the hummocky grass.

"What do you mean, *I'm* trespassing?" demanded Jane. She stared at the intruder, wishing he didn't have such mild, dreamy big eyes. "*You're* the one who's trespassing."

"What?"

"You heard," Jane said nastily.

The boy combed his mousy hair with nervous fingers. "But I can't be," he said uncertainly.

"I should know," Jane snarled. "I know where everyone lives round here. I live on the farm, look, over there, see? I've always lived there and I've never seen you before. Ever. So, where do *you* live, eh? Go on, show me."

"In that big house. I thought this field went with it ..."

"Fat lot you know, then," Jane said. Then she realised he was pointing directly at New House.

"Liar. You don't live there. No one lives there . . . now. It's . . . empty."

"Well, it won't be for much longer. We're moving in . . . any day now."

"Who's we?" Jane's voice trembled.

"Me and my – er – family."

Jane stared at the boy. "Who says?"

"That old man – who died – what's his name . . ."

"Mr Eliot." Jane felt too numb to rage against the boy's careless way of talking about her old friend.

"That's it. Sam Eliot. He was Nell's uncle and he left it to her. She's over the moon because our flat's so small. She wants to move in at once because . . ."

"But you can't, you can't," Jane burst in. "He's only just . . . died. It's too soon." She had not had even one short thought about what would happen to Mr Eliot's house and all his things.

"But you see," the boy was saying, "there's not much time because Nell's . . ."

"Who is Nell?" Jane interrupted.

"My stepmother."

"Oh." Jane didn't know what to say. And the boy turned away, looking about him. Both of them were uneasy, brought up against unspoken questions, explanations.

"Well, anyway," Jane urged after a moment. "What are you doing here all on your own?"

"Waiting for Nell – and I just thought I'd explore

a bit. It's smashing here. I can hardly wait to get out of smelly old London." He sounded excited, wanting to be friendly. But Jane took no notice.

"And what are you going to do when *Nell* gets here?" she asked sourly. "Where is she anyway?"

"She's gone to Castlebury, to see the lawyers. Then we're going to look over the house properly and sort things out for the sale."

"The *sale*?" Jane exploded.

"Yes," the boy nattered on. "She says the house is like a museum and a junk-shop rolled into one and we can't possibly live with so much clutter. I'm dying to choose my room."

Jane wasn't listening. The heavy truth that her freedom at New House was gone stuck thickly in her throat like lumpy semolina. Museum? Junk-shop? Sale? Her parents couldn't know about it or they would certainly have told her, warned her. I'm going to hate this Nell, Jane decided. Bet she'll keep the doors locked even when she's in. Huh! Jane felt fierce and shut as if she'd slammed a bolt on her own self.

And then she had a dreadful thought. "The dogs!" she squeaked.

"The what?"

"Nothing, nothing."

But it wasn't nothing. How could she have forgotten Large, Middling and Small? How would she ever get to play with them again? Suppose this Nell goes up to the attic? Of course she'll go up to the attic, and – and – find them, and – and sell them. She can't. I'll have to get them out. Somehow.

And hide them. Somewhere. I can always bring them back later. But how? How am I going to get them out? Even if I am polite and get asked in? How, how, how? When, when when?

"I hope Nell gets here soon." The boy broke into her worried thoughts. "I've left my Walkman in the car."

A dim idea crept up and took a feeble swipe at Jane's pride and secrecy. If she was nice to him perhaps he'd help her get the dogs out. See it as an adventure. "Walkman?" she heard herself say. "Lucky thing."

"Haven't you got one?" He sounded pitying.

"No, but I wish I had . . ." The dim idea faltered, backed off, turned tail, taking Jane with it. "My father says Walkmans turn you into wobbly zombies."

"Oh *my* dad's always saying things like that," the boy laughed. "Have you got an air gun?" He was gazing at the church spire.

"No."

"That weathercock looks as if someone has taken a pot shot at it. Did they?"

"I don't know," Jane said irritably. "It's always been like that." This stranger, this trespassing stranger was getting a bit too cheeky for her liking. She stared at the tilted weathercock. "Where's my hen?" she snapped.

"It's nesting in that little cupboard inside the little house." Jane shot up the ladder, longing to get away now and chew over a plan of rescue for the dogs. But the boy followed her, hounded her.

"Your boat's just like the ark, isn't it?"

"Yes."

"Why don't you fix it up? Why don't you launch it?"

"Why don't you shut up?" Jane covered her rude retort by making a terrific noise chasing the broody mother off her nest. "Go on! Shoo! shoo!" she yelled. The hen flapped onto the rail, teetered, then with an almighty squawk took off on the longest flight of her life, landed in the long grass and fled zig-zag homewards.

Jane squatted over the nest. "Five," she counted. "Five eggs. Bother! I should've brought a basket. I can't carry them all. Here, put out your hands." The boy obeyed and Jane gracelessly plonked two eggs into his palms. "Now follow me," she ordered.

"Tom! Tom! What on earth are you *doing* out there?"

Jane froze in her tracks. For the second time that morning a stranger's voice broke into her world.

"Oh good," cried the boy. "There's Nell. In the garden. With some old lady and a couple of kids."

"To-om! You're trespassing."

A smirk flitted across Jane's face: Tom, the trespasser. She knew his name now and he knew she'd been right. But so what? What did it matter? He was going to live at New House, come and go as he liked, more even than she'd ever done. He'd find the swing, sooner or later. Her time there was over. Over.

"To—om! We've got a lot to do. Come here at once!" called Nell.

"Twunce, Tom! Twunce!" echoed little Alice, bouncing up and down on Mrs Gurney's hip.

"I'm *coming*!" Tom yelled, already half-way down the ladder. Happy now he was no longer alone in a hostile land, he headed towards the open garden gate. "C'mon," he called jauntily over his shoulder. "Come and meet my wicked stepmother."

6 . Friend or Foe?

Nursing her eggs, her envy, her desperation about the dogs, Jane crept slowly towards the gate. She saw Tom put his eggs down in the flower-bed, say something to his stepmother and disappear round the corner. "Mean pig," Jane said under her breath. "He could've waited to introduce me. I should've gone straight home."

Pippa and Alice were swinging on the gate, hanging on tight with pudgy hands, squabbling over the cramped space, furtively treading on each other's little, wiggly summer-free toes.

"Jane Finch, Jane Finch," sang Pippa. "*You* can't come in."

"Can't cum-*in*," Alice agreed.

"Oh yes, she can, you little rascals! Hello Jane! I'm Nell Kingsley."

She was pretty. She was smiling. She was going to have a baby. Soon. Very, very soon.

Jane knew she was staring helplessly but now she understood, understood the hurry. But why hadn't Tom said? Come to think of it, perhaps he had. Or tried to. He'd said so many things and she had kept on butting in . . .

"You live at the farm, don't you?" Mrs Kingsley was asking.

"Yes." Jane broke the stare by putting her eggs down next to Tom's and wiping her hands on her skirt.

"Uncle Sam – Mr Eliot – often talked about you in his letters. You spent a lot of time together didn't you? Did lots of nice things together?"

"Yes." Jane was eager now to talk. "Yes, we played Monopoly . . . and . . ."

But Mrs Kingsley was rushing on. "Good," she smiled. "Good. I was just saying to Mrs Gurney I got held up . . ." But Jane had closed her ears. Why had she asked if she didn't really want to know? Shan't tell her about the marshmallows. Shan't tell her where he hid the toasting fork. But she couldn't stop bits of Mrs Kingsley's breathless sentences dropping into her: ". . . had to take . . . husband . . . airport . . . bad timing . . . always dashing off . . . then the lawyer! So wordy . . . pompous . . ."

"Alice! Pippa!" Mrs Gurney interrupted. "Come away from that pond. What a pair! Sorry, Mrs Kingsley. Back in a minute." She chased after the little girls, who were soon leading her a merry dance as they shot away from the pond and jerked, now here, now there, across the lawn like dragonflies.

Mrs Kingsley rubbed the small of her back and turned to Jane. "What have I let myself in for? In a year or so *I'll* be running all over this lawn with my own toddling rascal. Poor Mrs Gurney. They keep her on her toes, don't they? And it's so *hot*! Where *has* Tom got to? He's taking ages. He seems to be getting dreamier and slower by the day."

"I think he wanted his Walkman," said Jane.

Mrs Kingsley raised her eyebrows to the sky. "I know. I just hope he brings all the other things I asked him to fetch. There's so much to deal with I hardly know where to begin . . ."

Jane was beginning to feel sorry for Mrs Kingsley. She knew after all how funny hens get when they're nesting: fussing about with bits of straw and fluff. It was probably the same for her. She only wanted things ready and cosy for the baby. Jane wondered what it felt like to have a baby kicking inside you, decided she'd ask – not today, perhaps, but soon.

"Have you had any lunch?" asked Mrs Kingsley.

"N-n-no," stammered Jane.

Mrs Kingsley sighed. "I just wondered if you were as hungry as I am. That's what I sent Tom for – our sandwiches among other things. Why don't you join us for a bite? Ah, here he comes at last. Just look at him. In a complete dream?"

Round the corner came Tom. Wearing headphones, a Walkman clipped to his belt, he was walking crookedly, head in air, beating out some catchy rhythm and crooning to himself. Behind him a trail of paper gently fluttered from the carrier bags he was waving about in time to the music.

"Tom!" Mrs Kingsley shouted. "Oh Tom, *really*! Turn that thing off! You are the end! The labels!

The stickers! You're dropping everything, you idiot!"

But he couldn't hear.

Jane dashed forward, started to pick up the labels. Some were blue, some red, some white. Small black words reared up from all of them and hit her in the eye: *CHUCK*, they said, *KEEP*, *SELL*. Her pain began to burn. Mrs Kingsley seemed so nice, but they were her horrid labels. She'd planned them, written them, come here with them.

Then Jane knew, coldly, clearly, that she was ready to steal Large, Middling and Small from the attic. She wouldn't let them be *chucked*, or *sold* and certainly not *kept* by Mrs Kingsley with her sweet smile and her hasty, ungentle plans for the old house. Jane seethed in puzzlement. How can anyone smile like she does and be so – so – dark and snidey inside?

At that moment Pippa screamed and little Alice began to cry at the top of her voice. "Oh my goodness," wailed Mrs Gurney, who'd only turned away for a second, "Alice has been and gone and stuck some of those red berries up her nose."

All this noise even got through to Tom. He opened his half-closed eyes, stared around him, pulled off the headphones, gawped at Jane scrabbling over the labels, at Mrs Gurney flapping over Alice. "Oh lord," he said. "Sorry I've been so long, Nell, but there's such a mess in the car. I've got the sandwiches. I'm *starving*! Can we eat now?"

"Just a minute, Tom," cried Mrs Kingsley. "Just

a minute. Look at poor Mrs Gurney . . . and Jane."

"I'd best get these little ones home at once," Mrs Gurney said, "and get those berries out before she swallows 'em."

"They're rackling," Alice announced. She'd stopped crying and was tipping her head this way and that.

"Not rackling, silly," Pippa sniffed. "Rattling. Stay still or you'll *die*."

"Why don't you turn her upside down?" Jane suggested. The whole scene was beginning to feel like a mad dream.

"Yes!" screamed Pippa.

"No!" yelled Alice.

"Whatever made you say a thing like that, Jane Finch?" Mrs Gurney glowered at her. "Frightening the poor little thing. Now why don't *you* help Mrs Kingsley instead of me? You know the house every bit as well as I do, and it seems only polite that someone from here should welcome new-comers . . ."

"That's very sweet of you, Mrs Gurney," said Mrs Kingsley. She turned to Jane. "Would you, Jane? It would be so nice, such a help, to have someone familiar with the house while we sort things out. Stay – and have a sandwich with us, and then perhaps you could give Tom a hand with the labels.

"Yes." Jane agreed. "Yes, of course I'll help you. I'd like to very much."

"There's a good girl." Mrs Gurney turned away home. The dizzy din began to fade. Mrs Kingsley was already pushing at the half-open front door, prodding Tom through.

For a moment Jane stood still, clenching her fists. "I must think," she muttered. "I must be careful. I must be polite. I must be clever."

"Jane?" Mrs Kingsley beckoned. "Coming?"

Jane nodded and followed her into the house, cool and dark after the sun, quiet after the pandemonium in the garden and the busy noise of summer. Somehow she'd find a way to get the dogs out. Somehow.

7 . "Grace"

"The teapots will have to go," Mrs Kingsley declared. She'd kicked off her sandals and was cooling her toes on the kitchen flagstones. Tom had wolfed his sandwiches and begun to prowl round the huge room, mysterious in the half-light from its half-closed shutters.

"Marvellous teapots, but crazy!" she added. "Look, there's even one with two spouts and the lid itself another tiny teapot. You could pour tea for half an army from *one* of those, let alone three!"

The great brown teapots, encrusted with fat, cabbagy roses, bulged on the dresser. "But they'll have to go," Mrs Kingsley repeated, ticking them off her list. Jane sat on another chair, swinging her legs and flicking at crumbs from her last sandwich, trying to be calm, flick, careful, flick, clever, flick, flick.

"Tom," said Mrs Kingsley, "get the blue stickers – blue for sell. And just look at all these chairs! However many are there in this room?"

"Twenty," said Jane. They were ranged against the walls, clustered round the table. She pulled one over to the mantelpiece, swiftly climbed up and carefully down. "You'll keep this though, won't you?" she asked. Tenderly she held up a very

small, white teapot, patterned with deep blue garlands. *Grace*, it said on the lid, and *Grace* again in a circle of flowers on its side. 'Grace, born August eleventh, 1783 . . .' That's two hundred years ago – to the very day!"

"It's an omen," Tom intoned. "An o-o-men."

Mrs Kingsley laughed. "Don't be such an ass, Tom." She looked about her, for the first time letting the house's friendly oldness creep into her like a spell. "Perhaps it *is* an omen," she said quietly. "Although I'd call it a sign of welcome. 'Grace' ", she murmured, "an unasked-for present. A gift." She set the teapot down and smiled at Jane. "Pretty name – old-fashioned, but pretty. Perhaps it belonged to my great-great-great-grandmother. Of course I'll keep it! Red sticker, Tom!" She became brisk again. "And as for these chairs! The most we'll ever need is six."

Tom bounced about, fixing stickers accordingly. "Blue for sell, red for keep," he chanted over and over, as if he were playing a game. He doesn't care, Jane thought. He doesn't care who sat in these chairs, what words this room heard.

Mrs Kinglsey had wandered to the far corner of the kitchen. "What a dreadful old range! I'm not cooking on *that*!"

"Out of the ark," laughed Tom.

Jane shuddered, but clung to her vow to be polite. "It's got a back-boiler," she forced herself to say helpfully. "It does the radiators."

"Oh good," said Mrs Kingsley. "All the same, I'll bring my own cooker down."

"Hey, N-e-ell, come here a minute!" called Tom. He was kneeling on the floor. "Look, there's a ring in this stone." He began to tug at it. "Gosh, it's stiff. Wonder what it's for? Perhaps there's a tunnel under the floor."

"There isn't," said Jane.

"How do you know?" Tom demanded.

"Mr Eliot told me. He said there was a well there, once, a long time ago."

"But did he ever lift it up?" Tom argued. "Has anyone ever really looked? There might be a tunnel."

"Nonsense," said Mrs Kingsley, not really looking. That annoyed Jane. How did she know? How could she be so sure? Suddenly she found herself on the floor beside Tom. "I suppose there might be," she agreed.

"We'd need a crowbar to lift this stone." Tom wasn't going to give up too easily.

"Oh come on, you two," begged Mrs Kingsley. "Not now, whatever it is. Save it for a rainy day."

Jane and Tom scrambled slowly to their feet and trailed after her.

"First chance we get, will you help me?" whispered Tom.

"Mm . . . I might," Jane muttered.

"Your father will love this room," cried Mrs Kingsley, flinging open the door to the study. "Of course the walls will have to be stripped. I hate dingy varnish . . . that settle can stay. Can't you just see him, stretched out there with a brandy telling us about the tsetse? And there'll be room under that window for his desk and even space there for his slides and microscopes . . ."

"My dad's an entomologist," Tom bragged.

Tsetse? Ento-mologist? Jane felt sweaty in front of the unfamiliar words. She groped about in the dusty back shelves of her memory. Tsetse. Tsetse. – some very nasty fly, wasn't it? Something like that. Entomologist: someone interested in insects, wasn't it? A picture came to her of an untidy old man with trousers rolled to the knee running after a cabbage-white with a net. Something she must have seen in an ancient picture book?

"Oh," she said, cool, knowing. "Bugs."

"He travels all over the world doing research for international bodies." Tom stood there, proud of his father, and Jane giggled. She couldn't help it. Bugs and bodies. It sounded so funny.

Tom was angry, hurt. "If you're not careful," he snarled, "I won't let you get anywhere near that tunnel."

"I don't care about your silly tunnel," Jane hissed. But Mrs Kingsley's voice, still excited and flustered, washed over their battle.

"And all these books! I can't think about them now . . . but they'll have to be gone through sooner or later. Oh dear, my back is beginning to ache. Come on, Tom, let's leave this room for your father to play with. But we'll have that varnish off by Christmas and the door stripped – all the doors stripped, perhaps. What do you think?"

Jane turned away. *Chuck, keep, strip, sell*. Barking, hurried words, so they sounded to her.

Tom just grunted. "This is all taking ages," he moaned. "I'm thirsty. I want an iced *coke* and you said I could go swimming . . ."

"In a minute, in a minute . . ." Mrs Kingsley's voice floated from the sitting-room. "Ohh!," she wailed. "We can't live in a museum. We just can't. These chairs and cabinets, that chest! They're all collectors' pieces." At last Jane agreed with Mrs Kingsley about something. She had never felt easy in this elegant room, nervously passing sherry round at Christmas time.

"They'll all have to go." Mrs Kingsley was stabbing wildly at her notebook. "We'll have to bring down our old sofa and chairs and the old blue carpet. Lovely curtains . . . and those rugs! But much too good for boys and babies, mud and biscuit crumbs!"

"And cat's hairs," Tom added.

"And cat's hairs," his stepmother agreed. "We've got this gangster of a one-eyed tomcat," she explained.

"But suppose he runs away?" Tom asked. "Cats hate new places."

"Lucky won't run away from paradise," Mrs Kingsley said firmly. "All those juicy mice and birds."

"And rabbits," Jane put in. She felt forsaken. Room by room, Tom and his stepmother were 'moving in', getting much too private and cosy. "*Our* cat eats rabbits – *whole*."

"Good heavens!" cried Mrs Kingsley, and buried her head again in her notebook. She didn't see

Tom mouth 'liar' at Jane, shove his hands in his pockets and slink off down the wide passage. She didn't see Jane shrug and stick her tongue out at his back.

"Right!" Mrs Kingsley snapped her notebook shut. "Blue stickers for all this lot, Tom! To-om? Now where are you?" she groaned.

"In here, Nell," came the answer. "Come and see! Come and see this!"

"This way," said Jane. Best to get it over. She knew Tom had found the heart of the house, Mr Eliot's den: the fireplace small and cosy, its mantel-piece jutting out laden with treasures; the walls of faded pink; a window-seat you could snuggle into and shroud yourself in its heavy brown curtains; a door leading straight into the orchard full of bent old apple and quince trees, a short-cut to the swing. A battered armchair faced a rocking chair across the fireplace. Books, board games, playing cards lay jumbled and tumbled on shelves in an alcove. And in the corner lay Jane's garden on its wobbly table. It was her pride and joy: the two tiny spruce trees Mr Eliot had given her, little pebbles, mossy hillocks – and – the pond, a deep delicate shell made from some tarnished metal, scalloped round the rim. It held the water like a seaside pool. The smallest shell she'd ever found glistened in its depths.

"What a dreadful old hidey-hole," Mrs Kingsley quavered. "I've never seen such a load of old junk. What am I going to do with it all?" She sank into the armchair and closed her eyes. "Really, I could cry."

Jane *was* crying. Dreadful? Junk? Is that how a stranger saw this gentle room with a story, a memory behind every object? And now there was Tom nosing his way along the mantelpiece. She couldn't bear it. She would go home. Now. At once. And later she'd come back and steal the dogs. Steal. 'Call a spade a spade' her father always said. So she'd be a thief. She didn't care. Jane headed blindly for the door, clogged up with tears and, of course, no handkerchief.

"Ne-ell, it's not dreadful. It's not junk." Tom was thoroughly indignant. "It's smashing. It's the best room by far. Look at these super old models! A Rolls and a Sopwith Camel and all these sailing ships. Must've taken hours of work."

Jane stopped in her tracks. She couldn't believe her ears! Tom! Now they were two! Two against one. She moved towards him. Oh yes! She'd help him to look for the tunnel. Tell him so in a minute. "And look at this hour-glass," he was saying. He tipped it over and set the thin line of sand trickling, then stood it carefully again in its place.

"There are toffees in that goblet," Jane said, "and dice. And buttons. He – he put them there when they fell off his shirts."

"Spillikins," said Tom.

"Pipecleaners."

"One of those Chinese puzzle things. I love them. And who made the garden?"

"I did." Jane's tears began to fall again.

"Nell," called Tom. "Come and look at this. It's really nice. Jane made it." He looked at Jane and quickly away again. "Don't be an ass. Everything's going to be all right."

"Yes, Jane." Mrs Kingsley was suddenly beside her, her arm round her. "I'm sorry. I'm really, really sorry. It must have been awful for you, us appearing out of the blue, and especially among all the things that remind you of the happy times you've had in this house. I simply wasn't thinking. Tell you what. We'll leave it all for now – all – just as it is. We'll lock the doors till after the sale. Then you can choose anything you like – anything – and take it home."

"I think Tom should have the models and the games and the puzzle," Jane sniffed.

"You could set up your garden again in *The Ark*," Tom suggested. "I'll help you."

"Yes," Mrs Kingsley agreed. "It's only right that you should have something to remember Uncle Sam by. Good lord!" she clapped her hand to her mouth. "I've just remembered! How could I have forgotten? Uncle Sam *did* leave you something. I was supposed to tell you . . . The attic!"

A thousand butterflies rose and fell in Jane's stomach.

"Some dogs – in the attic – is that right?" Mrs Kingsley clasped her forehead.

"Dogs?" laughed Tom.

"China dogs, silly," said Jane.

"Yes. That's it." Mrs Kingsley was relieved. "Uncle Sam wanted you to have three china spaniels you were very fond of and they're stored in the attic!"

Jane could not stand still another second.

"C-c-can I?"

"Yes, go on. Off you go. Tom, give her a hand. We won't do any more today. I think we've all had more than enough."

Jane ran to the door and then back again. "Grace," she said.

"What?"

"You know. Grace – what you said. An unasked-for present. This house, your teapot, my . . . the dogs?"

"Yes. Yes. That's right. That's quite right. Which reminds me. I must rescue my 'Grace' from the kitchen and then, Jane, do you think your mum would give us a cup of tea?"

8 . Storm Clouds

"C'mon, Jane," Mrs Finch urged. "At least get him to *trot*! He's getting as fat as butter, and I must say Tweedledum's not much better. Just as well for *you*," she turned to Tom. "He's not likely to take off like a bat out of hell. Now, remember what I said. Straight back! Reins slack. And grip! Grip with your knees!"

Jane nudged Tweedledee into a half-baked gallop, overtook the others, slowed down again.

It had seemed such a good idea, hatched between her mother and Nell Kingsley over tea at the end of that long, strange day. Tom should come to stay while his stepmother went back to London to pack up and get the move under way. Of course he should stay. Jane had been so happy, lying on the lawn, drinking Coke with Tom; the dogs, her dogs now, sitting obediently at her feet. But now she could hardly wait for him to leave. Today he was moving into New House with his parents where they would camp out till the sale was over. Tom had already chosen his room. The best one, of course, the one Jane would have chosen, the one with the friendly, leaning tree you could shin up and down unseen at any time of day or night. He had made endless little sketches of the room and

where he would put all his things. And when he wasn't doing anything else he'd fiddled and struggled till he'd solved Mr Eliot's Chinese puzzle, which he now kept all the time in his pocket.

Jane felt like she did at country dancing. Giddy. Always arriving, puffed out, to find a new partner. Tom shy, Tom bored, Tom dreamy, Tom whiny. And now Tom bossy, excited, cocky, edging her out. One Tom but at the same time twenty Toms. Just like country dancing and changing partners too quickly.

She turned in the saddle, watched her mother prod Tom's sagging back, teasing him, gently bullying him. It had been like this every day for over a week. Every morning she tagged along while Tom had his riding lesson. Every afternoon she helped scrape down *The Ark*'s flaky hull until she'd had enough of Tom's bouncy enthusiasm. Then she'd skulk off to collect eggs, wipe eggs, pack eggs, make daisy chains or sea-shell bracelets for the little girls.

Where was the Tom who'd stuck up for the den, admired her garden, told her not to cry, helped her to carry the dogs, so carefully, down from the attic, the Tom who'd wanted her to help him explore a tunnel?

Jane sighed. What had she imagined? That you could make real friends with someone in a single day? A day that had started off so badly? No, he was a stranger, who for a short moment had been her ally. A cajoling stranger who had enticed them all down to *The Ark*, and when Mr Finch saw that the timbers were seaworthy, had them all in the Land Rover and off to Castlebury before you could say 'knife' to buy scrapers and gallons of paint. He hadn't touched his Walkman for days. He had forgotten all about the tunnel. He whistled toneless tunes of joy. He was chatty. Pippa and Alice were always after him. Daisy chains scattered, sea shells spilled, "Tom," they'd call. "Tom, Tom Piper's son! Carry! Carry! Piggy-back! Piggy-back!" You'd think he was some magic creature fallen from the sky specially for them. They squabbled over who should ride on his back, moaned that Jane didn't carry so well, couldn't run so fast. Flattered and boisterous, it seemed to Jane that Tom really thought he was king of the castle.

"Jane," called her mother. "Stop day-dreaming, darling. You and Tweedledee look as if you'd turned to stone. Now, why don't you take Tom down to Darting Mill? He won't have much time for frolics once that sale's over. It's lovely down there and it's time Tom got to know the lie of the land. You could take a picnic. Enough of horses and boats for a bit. You might even see the king-fisher! Come on! Let's get these saddles off and make some huge cheese-and-tomato sandwiches. Fresh tomatoes, picked this morning." Mrs Finch smiled at her daughter. Jane felt like kissing her. She understood. She was trying to help, help her get used to these new days, help her to let a new pattern grow.

The great trees in the water-meadow shimmered

in the sun and a heron rose from the river as they trudged along the bank that led towards Darting Mill, curving past the railway track.

"Have you ever seen a kingfisher?" Jane asked Tom. Her mother's parting words still whispered in her: *Please darling, be good. Just for a few more hours.*

"Nope," said Tom, picking up a stick and flicking hard at the reeds.

"I have, but only three times in my whole life. It's fantastic! A quick flash and it's gone. You think you've dreamed it."

"So? What's the big deal?"

"It's the blue of it, the speed of it! The luck of it. Just to catch a glimpse. Ohh! You'd know if you saw one," Jane ended irritably.

"I'm not into bird-watching," Tom slashed at the reeds.

"That's not bird-watching," scoffed Jane. "That's – that's catching sight of – of – magic."

"You're soppy, you know," sneered Tom. "Did anyone ever tell you that? You are soppy."

Again her mother's voice haunted Jane: *Please darling, be good.* She needed a moment to pull herself together. "My sandal's come undone," she said. She knelt down and fiddled with the buckle. "I'll catch you up in a minute."

But Tom didn't walk on. He towered above her on the bank, hands on hips, surveying his new kingdom. His eye fell on the railway line, then moved to a small bridge the trains passed over.

"The rails are humming," said Tom. "A train's

coming. Race you to that bridge! There must be a terrific din under there when a train's going over. Come on then, soppy, what are you waiting for? Not scared are you?"

"No," said Jane defiantly. "I've done it before. Lots of times. It's – it's – boring."

"Oh, I see," said Tom. "Boring is it? Well, I haven't done it before, so I'm going to do it now, see? And if you won't race me, I'll race the train instead. I didn't ask to come on this nature walk, you know." And just as the train came round the bend he tore down the slope and disappeared under the bridge.

Jane's heart lurched as she stared at the black hole and an old fear poured into her. When she was very small her brother had dragged her in there just as a train was thundering overhead like a monstrous metal centipede. The noise was terrifying. Toby had stood there yelling his head off, enjoying some kind of competition with the machine. She had cowered for what seemed like a hundred years against the glistening, mouldering wall, its nasty wetness seeping through her dress, begging him, unheard, to get her out of there. How he had teased her on the way home. And now here was Tom coming back with a sneer on his face. It was like the re-play of an old bad dream.

"That was great," said Tom. "What a fantastic din. I yelled my head off. You couldn't say that was boring. I think you were scared. Were you? Were you scared? Eh, poor little Jane?"

"No I was not," snapped Jane. "I just happen not to like dark, damp, noisy places."

"Oh, you're no fun," said Tom. "No fun at all. Just soppy."

"Don't keep saying that!" snarled Jane.

Tom began to dance along the path in front of her. "Kingfishers are magic! The *blue* of it," he taunted and mimicked.

Now rage overpowered Jane. "I wish you'd never come here," she yelled. "You've made everything horrible. Horrible. I'm not going anywhere with you. Anywhere. Ever. You can fetch your beastly things and your beastly Walkman and get off our land. And keep off my *Ark*, do you hear? Trespasser. Bossy boots. Towny. Towny. I'm glad you're leaving today anyway." Jane turned away, her voice juddering with anger and tears. "Horsey boy. Horsey. Horsey. I hope you have a really achey bum tonight and tomorrow night . . . and . . . and . . . You'll never find that tunnel, you know. You'll never find it. Because it isn't there, see? It isn't there. Don't just stand there with your mouth open, unless you want to swallow flies. Here, take your sandwiches and go away. Go away. I never want to see you again."

And she threw down the sandwiches, stumbled across the water-meadow into the farm garden and flung herself down under the mulberry tree, seething, like some nasty soup made by witches, about to boil over in the cauldron.

9 . Bees in their Bonnets

"I must say, I'm surprised at Tom," Mrs Finch said next morning. "Sneaking off yesterday without saying goodbye. Just leaving a note. Very peculiar."

"Oh, you know boys at that age," Mr Finch replied. "Probably didn't know what to say to you face to face."

"Don't go on about it, Mum," Jane added.

"You two didn't have a row, I suppose?" Mrs Finch persisted.

"No, of course we didn't." At least Jane and Tom seemed to agree about one thing: to keep quiet about their terrible quarrel.

"Did you see the kingfisher?" Mrs Finch asked. "I quite forgot to ask you last night what with Mrs Gurney getting in such a state about Pippa's wasp sting . . ."

"No, we didn't," said Jane.

"Never mind. It's always sheer luck. Next time, perhaps. Are you coming to the sale?"

"I – I'd rather not," Jane admitted.

"Oh, darling," pleaded Mrs Finch. "I think you should. At least come over for a few minutes. Otherwise the Kingsleys'll think you're sulking."

"Yes, Jane," her father agreed. "I think you should at least come and say hullo to Tom's dad. You haven't met him yet, have you? And, you know, you've got to get used to the changes round here."

Jane just couldn't tell them that she was scared of meeting Tom; that the quarrel had even overpowered her feelings about the changes at New House. They'd only interfere and talk to his parents about it.

"All right," she said. "I'll come – for a bit."

"That's the girl." Mr Finch gave her a hug. "Well, go on then. Go and brush your hair, mophead!"

But Jane forgot about Tom when she saw the crowd in the kitchen: strangers, slightly sinister in dark suits; girls in long bright skirts wearing dangly ear-rings; women twittering like sparrows, peering, almost pecking at the stacks of china and glass Jane had never seen before. Her father introduced her to Robin Kingsley. He didn't wear his trousers rolled, and he wasn't carrying a butterfly net. He was very tall and thin, like a dreamy stick insect. He shook hands with her. "Sorry Tom isn't here," he said. "He's loafing about down by the river with his precious Walkman. Said this kind of thing wasn't his 'scene'."

"Oh, oh yes, I see." Jane heaved a sigh of relief and waved to Nell Kingsley talking to her mother. "What a lot of things!"

"It is rather overpowering, isn't it?" Robin Kingsley agreed. "I'll leave you to wander, shall I?" Jane nodded gratefully and moved away between the hordes of chairs and heavy-laden trestle tables. She gazed upwards. The old clothes rack, hoisted close to the range, was draped with embroidered linen and silks from other age.

Mrs Gurney came up to her blowing her nose. "Oh, Jane, I didn't know they was getting rid of all them lovely things . . ."

"Is Pippa all right now?" Jane asked abruptly. *She* wasn't going to cry.

"What? Oh yes, my dear. I've left her napping and Alice playing as good as gold with my old man."

"Where does all this stuff come from?" Jane asked. "There's a lot I've never seen before."

Mrs Gurney waved at shadowy cupboards and chests of drawers which Jane had always walked straight past, her eyes only for the jolly teapots, the warm range, marshmallows and her dear old friend.

"Washed and shined," Mrs Gurney intoned. "Washed and starched Easter and Michaelmas these forty years. I can't bear to see them go. Ending up in that Portobelly Market, I dare say."

Jane would like to have comforted her, but Mrs Gurney had become stiff, prickly. She gave Jane a sharp nudge. "Look at them. There's that Mrs Pobjoy from Castlebury and all them hippies pushing and shoving. They should go back where they belong – wherever that is. It's just like the sales. The vultures!"

"Quite right, Mrs Gurney," came a mournful voice, "only I call 'em piranhas. Dealers! Piranhas of the trade, that's what I call 'em. Snap up all the goodies. Tough on us small businessmen . . ."

"Why, it's Scully! Scully Jenkin." Mrs Gurney began to cheer up. "I might have know you couldn't keep away today . . ."

Scully Jenkin nodded at Jane. She recognised the wiry man. He was the owner of Jenkin's Curiosities next to the fish shop in Castlebury market-place. He must have seen her nose a thousand times, pressed against the grubby window of his shop, seen her eyes yearning after the hand-painted toy theatre tilted among his boring bric-à-brac. His shifty eyes wandered upwards to the snowy forest hanging from the ceiling and down again to the paper-thin Chinese cups and saucers, the pretty pearly fish knives.

"Still," he said more brightly. "I might just pick up one or two nice little things." He winked at Jane. "Theatre's still there. Don't dilly-dally, don't shilly-shally. Summer visitors, you know. Like gulls. Swoop down on things when it's too rainy to go to the beach. Here today, gone tomorrow."

"I wish I could have it," Jane said, "but you can't do plays on your own."

"You'll have to find a *play*mate," advised Mr Jenkin. "A *play mate*," he repeated, inviting her to laugh at his little pun.

But Jane didn't laugh. Standing in that noisy room, surrounded by greedy grown-ups, she simply thought of Tom skulking down by the river with his Walkman. Tomorrow, she vowed to herself, tomorrow, first thing, I'll say sorry.

"Still bell-ringing over at St Mary's, Scully?" inquired Mrs Gurney.

Scully's face lit up like a Hallowe'en pumpkin with a bright new candle in it. "Of course!" he cried. "Of course! Once a bell-ringer always a bell-ringer."

"I'm glad you still ring them, Scully," said Mrs Gurney.

"I know what you're thinking," said Scully, "but so long as I hang on to the bells – hang on, eh?" He looked hopefully to see if they'd noticed his joke. "There'll be hope for me when I go knocking at the pearly gates." He disappeared into the other room.

"He looks like a crook," said Jane.

"Next best thing, I fear," Mrs Gurney sighed. "He always was a naughty little tyke. But the bells! How he loves the bells. They'll keep him on the straight and narrow. Oh yes, I trust the bells."

"Stone the crows!" Jane exploded. "People are funny!"

" 'Course they are, my dear, 'course they are – and you watch your tongue. What sounds all right on my old man's lips doesn't sound altogether right coming from yours . . . 'Course people are funny. We've all got bees in our bonnets. Take my old man and his orchids. He'd give his all for them, or a sickly lamb come to that, but he won't weed the garden, will he . . . ? And I'm no better," Mrs Gurney confided. "Sad I am at this sale, but I love an outing, I love a crowd, I like a little niggle about other folks . . ."

"And what about me then?" Jane asked.

"You?" Mrs Gurney laughed. "You're an April Day if ever there was one, and have been since the day you was born. There's two sides to every penny and more than two to folk, I dare say."

Tom, Jane called silently. *Tom, I'm sorry.*

"Now look at that, Jane," Mrs Gurney prattled on. "What would Mrs Pobjoy want with a teapot that size? She's only got herself to pour for. Never asks a neighbour in."

Mrs Pobjoy's knobbly fingers were stretching out towards the pot with the two spouts.

"Madam, *please*," begged an elderly man, clasping his hands in distress. "Please, please don't touch. They're destined for the *museum*." His false teeth whistled mightily at every passing 's'.

"Don't fret, Mr Knowles," Mrs Pobjoy snapped. "I was only *looking* . . ."

"Huh!" Mrs Gurney sniffed. "Oops! That linen's slipping off the rack." She bustled off to the rescue.

"Very fine pieces," Mr Knowles said to Jane at his elbow. "Very fine. Hope to add them to my – er – *the* collection, you know. You know my – er – *the* museum in Castlebury, of course. You *know* our teapots, do you?"

"Yes," said Jane. "I went with the school. I liked the cauliflower one best – you know, the one with all the veins showing in the leaves and the little white bits – just like a real cauliflower – brilliant!"

"Yes. Yes. Good – er – good." smiled the tufty-haired old man, "I don't myself know the teapots individually, but I'm told it's the finest collection in the country," he continued. "My speciality is ecclesiastical plate." And now his whistling was so mighty that Jane had to throttle back the first gurgle of laughter she'd felt for ages.

"What is 'a clesi-elastical' plate?" she asked.

"Church gold, church silver, crosses, chalices, patens and so on and so forth . . ." sang Mr Knowles.

"Oh. I see." Jane wasn't interested and began to wonder how she could get away from the talkative curator. But he hadn't finished with her yet.

"You live hereabouts, do you?" inquired Mr Knowles.

"On the farm. I was born here."

"Ah, a Map's End child." His voice had grown mysterious. "So you'll have heard the story of Master Piers?"

"Master Piers?" Jane echoed.

"Who lived in this very house long, long ago," Mr Knowles droned on, "forging from gold – and silver – the most glorious ecclesiastical plate." His teeth whistled again into top gear.

Oh dear, Jane said to herself, *another one with a bee in his bonnet*.

"N-no," she spluttered. "N-n-never heard of him."

"Really?" cried the old man. "Dear me, dear me. No sense of the past about any more. No continuity. No feeling of *heritage*." He shook his head; then shook himself. "Knowles!" he commanded. "Don't be such a fuddy-duddy! Church plate is hardly something to excite the interest of a . . . young person. Now if it was pieces-of-eight it would be another story, eh?"

"Pieces-of-eight?" Jane caught the words and brightened up at once. "What about pieces-of- . . . ?"

"Ladies and gentlemen, ladies and gentlemen! May I have your attention, please!"

Space suddenly cleared and a brisk man appeared behind a tall wooden stand, holding a small wooden mallet.

"The auctioneer," Mr Knowles whispered. "I must certainly pay attention. No treasure, but I mustn't let the teapots slip from my grasp . . ."

"Right," said the auctioneer. "Let's see how quickly we can get this lot under the hammer."

"The brute." Jane winced and slipped quietly away home, half afraid, half-hoping she might meet Tom on the way. "Tomorrow," she promised herself. "Tomorrow I'll say sorry."

10 . Message in a Bottle

But when tomorrow came Jane wished she hadn't waited. Her feet no longer urged her to rush off in search of Tom. They were as heavy as nuggets of bullion. She knew in a different way from yesterday she must say sorry to him, but she didn't feel the same about it. She dawdled over breakfast, picking at her toast; she dawdled making her bed; dawdled in the garden and then, when at last she stolidly set out for New House, she found the doors all locked and the car gone. The Kingsleys had vanished. Instead of being glad she didn't have to choke just yet over that small word 'sorry', she was furious. How much longer would she have to go round feeling as if some terrible old monster was hanging on her back throttling the life out of her? What if they'd gone out for the whole day? And got back really late?

She stomped home, but when she strode into the kitchen she found her father still sitting at the table, fiercely stirring his coffee. Round and round went the spoon. Clink, clink. And the coffee swirled about faster and faster like a savage whirlpool. Her mother had her back to them, staring out of the window, blowing her nose.

"Oh Jim!" she cried, spinning round crossly. "For heaven's sake, stop it! Stop that awful racket! Oh there you are, Jane darling." Her eyes were red and watery and she spoke as if she had a cold. "I was just coming to look for you . . ."

"What's happened?" Jane cried. "Where's Tom?"

"Tom's fine," said her father. "His dad just phoned to tell us he's packed Tom off . . ."

"Why?" Jane demanded. "Why?" It couldn't be because of her, could it? Or could it?

"Nell had her baby," said Mrs Finch calmly. "Last night."

"Oh, but that's too soon!" Jane protested. "She said another six weeks . . ."

"I know," said her mother. "It happened late last night. She suddenly went into labour – too much excitement, I expect – and they rushed her to Castlebury Hospital."

"Is it all right?" quavered Jane. "It isn't – dead – is it?"

"No," said her mother, "but it's having some difficulty breathing . . . It's very, very small, you see . . ."

"*She*," put in her father sternly. "Not *it*. She. A little girl."

"A girl?" repeated Jane. "Will she be all right?"

"She's in an incubator," said Mrs Finch. "Having a rough start, poor tiny little thing."

"Oh," Jane gasped. "How awful. Poor baby. Poor Kingsleys, poor Tom. Where is he? Who's looking after *him*?"

"Robin Kingsley is with Nell at the hospital and

Tom's gone to his grandparents. He hoped, if things improve, that he and Tom would be back here before long getting the house ready and coming and going to the hospital."

"Try not to get too upset, darling," said her mother.

"They can do wonders these days with premature babies," Mr Finch added.

"I know," Jane admitted. She turned to her mother. "Shall we take Tweedledum and Tweedle-dee out for a bit?" She wanted to stay near someone but not to talk any more.

"Good idea," said her father, "and I must get a move on. Got to go into Castlebury to see the bank manager." He pulled a gloomy face.

"Can you wait? Just *one* sec?" Jane begged. "If I quickly pick some flowers you could leave them at the hospital, couldn't you?"

"I suppose so," agreed her father.

"It's hardly the moment, is it," asked her mother, "to shower the Kingsleys with a great bunch of flowers?"

"Then just one rosebud," pleaded Jane. "Just one of those little white ones for the baby. Nell can keep it for her by her bed."

"I think that's a great idea," said Mr Finch.

"Go on, then," said Mrs Finch. "But hurry up! Your dad hasn't got all day!"

Jane enjoyed the amble on her tubby pony down to the river bank. The flowing water and the shimmering alders quieted her. She felt ready to be on her own again.

"That was nice," she said to her mother as they hung up their tack in the dark stable.

"Good." Mrs Finch smiled. "Now, how about a sandwich and a cool drink before I make some ice-cream for supper?"

"Do you mind if I take mine down to *The Ark*? I'd like to start cleaning up the inside so that when Tom gets back we can really get on with the last bit of painting."

"Right you are," agreed Mrs Finch. "And if you bring those grubby old curtains in later we could give them a wash."

But when Jane sat down in the stuffy cabin to eat her sandwiches, she didn't feel hungry any more. She no longer wanted to be busy. She couldn't stop herself from thinking of the baby in its incubator. She'd seen pictures on television of tiny, naked babies connected up to tubes and gadgets, all wrinkled and puckered. It must be awful for the parents and – and the brother, even if he was only a half-brother. It was horrible to know that there was nothing she could do to help, that, like them, she'd just have to wait and pray, wait and keep her fingers crossed, her toes crossed. She fiddled with pencil and paper and got out her pastel chalks. She could make the Kingsleys a beautiful card, but what kind of card? It couldn't be a get-well card, or a good luck card or a congratulations card. It would only make them sad if . . . if . . . the baby . . . if the baby didn't get better.

Jane put her pencil down and stared gloomily

round the cabin. Large, Middling and Small stared back from their new home on the bench. Large and Middling, lofty as ever, stared through her, past her, above troubling themselves with the sorrows of humans, but, as usual, Small seemed to catch her eye eagerly, affectionately.

One by one Jane picked them up and laid them carefully down on the table in front of her. She fished out some sticky wine gums from Middling's hollow insides and popped one into her mouth. "I wish you'd come to life," she said to Small, sucking sweet black juice. She could have sworn in the dim light she saw his tail wag. "Jane Finch, don't be daft," she told herself and began to grope in Large's innards, not quite sure after so long what she had hidden in there. She nearly put her blind finger through the wren's egg nestling in the pheasant feathers. Then she remembered Dumpy, her doll, and the shells. They must have slipped right to the back of the hollow, deadpan dog. She wriggled her finger about in all the dark directions until it touched something she didn't remember putting there: something taped to the dog's inside, round, hard, papered, ridged with string. A parcel. A very small parcel. Who on earth had put it there? Someone with the nimble fingers of a model-maker? Her stomach lurched like it did in lifts. With sudden excitement she hooked her finger under the unknown parcel and nudged it slowly, clumsily nearer the opening. She lifted Large and began to shake him, trying to gauge where the parcel was so that she could get it to drop gently

out of the hole. At last it worked. The parcel plopped out and began to roll along the table. Quickly Jane put her hand over it. Held it neatly in her palm. *For Jane*, it said, in steady old-fashioned writing. Jane trembled. One person and one person only could have given her this surprise: one person only had known the secret of the dogs and passed it on to her. He had not forgotten her. She sighed.

He must have climbed all those stairs to the attic one more time for her. She untied the small neat knot with shaky hands and uncurled the paper. In her hand lay a bottle, a very small bottle, stopped up with a sliver of cork. Through the smoky glass she saw a minute scroll of paper.

"It's from him," she confided to Small. "It's a present from Mr Eliot. It's my message, my message in a bottle." And did Small's head nod in the dim light? Was this all magic?

She had her finger on the cork when her mother called, and Pippa called and Alice called.

"Ja-ane! How about the *cur*tains?"

"Ja-ane! Ja-ane!

"Out-and-out-a-*cur*tins?"

Jane stroked the little bottle. She could wait. Oh yes. She'd enjoy the wait. Till bedtime when she could shut herself up in her room, and then . . . and then . . ."

"Coming!" she called.

She could wait. She could wash curtains. She could play with Pippa and Alice while all the time her message in a bottle burned a happy hole in her deepest, most secret pocket.

11 . Joining
      In

"I think I'll go to bed really early," said Jane as she
licked up the last of her third helping of raspberry
ice-cream.

"Good idea," agreed Mr Finch. "It's been quite a
day!"

"Yes," Mrs Finch agreed, trying to thread a
needle in the fading summer light. "What a laughing, golden afternoon! Though, by the end of it, I
was beginning to feel the Wild Things had come
to stay."

"Why is your sewing maching hanging out of
the sitting-room window, so to speak?" asked Mr
Finch.

"Because *The Ark*'s curtains fell to pieces in the
wash, dear. They were rotten, quite rotten."

"I see," said Mr Finch.

"So Mum decided to make some new ones at
once," Jane explained.

"I see," said her father.

"But I couldn't bear to stay indoors on such a
lovely day, so I dragged the flex out through the
window and set myself up on the lawn."

"She looked so funny," Jane added, "in her old
hat with the brim bumping into the machine every

time she bent over it and going all skew-whiff."

"But she wouldn't take it off?" asked her father.

"Certainly not," Mrs Finch protested. "Didn't want to get sunstroke!"

"And she tried to teach me *hemming*," said Jane.

"But of course she refused to wear a thimble . . ."

"So I pricked my finger . . ."

"And the little girls screamed . . ."

"At the sight of three drops of blood . . . Like in Snow White . . ."

"So Jane took them for rides in the wheelbarrow to calm them down . . ."

"And that's why the grass cuttings aren't raked up and on the compost heap?" asked Mr Finch.

"Mm," said Jane. "And then we played He till Mrs Gurney came to put them to bed and told me off for letting them go all wriggly and giggly."

"Can you blame her?" asked Mr Finch.

"Not really," Jane agreed.

A menacing winged cloud swooped past the open window. Jane pictured the field mice cowering in the long grass and feared for them.

"I wish there was some news," she sighed, bringing out into the open what had been near them all through the hot still day. Her hand closed over the little bottle. Because of her secret she had more room than ever now for thoughts about the helpless baby.

"No news is good news," said her mother, snipping off her thread.

"Is that true?" Jane asked.

"No, not always," Mrs Finch admitted, "but

often, very often, it is. Promise! Now, go on! Off to bed with you and, darling, put the light on as you go!"

Jane closed her door and switched on the lamp. She sat down at the table in front of her window, and drew the bottle from her pocket. The cork came out with a whispered pop. She winkled out the small scroll with her finger-tips. Then she waited for a second. A message. A message from Mr Eliot. What would it be?

Greedy now, she quickly undid the folds one by one, laid the tiny sheet of paper on the table and bent closer to the lamp to read what was written there. A huge question mark leapt out at her, set in a whirligig of gobbledygook.

She turned the paper this way and that. A jumble of letters and numbers and what looked like a bunch of musical notes unwound themselves before her flabbergasted eyes. She put the paper down and groaned. A last joke? Most surely not: he'd said he laughed with her, not at her. She glared at the taunting question mark, at the maddening, crazy spiral. "It's a code," she muttered. "A horrid code. But . . that's not like Mr Eliot! He knew I was hopeless at sums and word games! Look what happened whenever we tried to play Scrabble or chess! So why? Why would he do a thing like that to me? Why? He must have known I'd never be able to work it out by myself. By myself," Jane repeated. "Oh, so that's it. That's the message. Ask for help. Ask for help. Ohhh, stone the flaming crows . . . I remember . . ."

And suddenly she was back at the beach. She felt the sand between her toes, the sun hitting her between her shoulder-blades. She heard the coming and going of the sea. She heard Mr Eliot's voice: *Join in, my dear, join in.* She pieced together again that day and the patchwork of her moods. Then she was back in her room, alone in the summer night, with an empty bottle, a sliver of cork and a message she didn't understand.

She looked at the riddle again, the tantalising whorl of mixed ciphers. Who could help her? Her parents? She could see it now: the three of them sitting down methodically after the table had been cleared and wiped free of crumbs. How dull, how daylightish. Mrs Gurney? Jane had often seen her toiling and moiling over the egg-packing accounts, sighing loudly, licking her pencil. Mrs Gurney treated letters and numbers like summer trippers: kept them at the frostiest possible distance. Well, Mr Gurney then? But he was forever on his orchid hunt and she didn't even know if he was any good at puzzles.

Puzzles. Tom. Of course. It must be Tom. She'd seen how he'd struggled with that Chinese puzzle, slotting and re-slotting all the little pieces until they fitted perfectly. Somehow saying sorry to him fitted here too. Of course he was the person she wanted to help her, to share the mystery of the message.

The snake-like question mark teased her in the shrinking light. *No ideas? No ideas at all? No pattern showing? No clue? Bad luck! You'll have to wait then, won't you? You'll have to wait for Tom.* Jane groaned. "I can't bear it. Oh, I wish he'd come home!"

She stared at the shadowy New House with all her might, willing Tom home, wishing Tom home. And when, after three minutes, the light went on in his bedroom, Jane felt all-powerful. With shaking hands she folded the scrap of paper and tucked it back into the bottle, stoppered it, crept barefoot downstairs past the sitting-room where the ten o'clock news was blaring out and shot across the dewy, cooling grass to the bottom of Tom's tree.

"Tom," she hissed, not daring to shout in case his father heard. "Tom."

No answer. And no good throwing stones because the window on this baking night was wide open.

"Perhaps he's gone to clean his teeth," Jane said to herself, and promptly began to shin up the friendly, leaning tree. She stopped just below the sill and called again.

"Tom! Tom! Are you there?"

A startled, tousled Tom almost fell out of the window. "Jane? Jane! Is that you? I was just having a cold bath." He sounded excited, pleased to see her.

"I saw your light."

"And I saw yours. I was dying to talk to you, but thought I'd better wait till morning. The baby's better . . . Coming on fine, they said tonight."

"Oh good," breathed Jane.

"She's tiny," said Tom. "Absolutely tiny. Not much more than two kilos."

"Like a small bag of new potatoes," said Jane. Tom laughed.

"A little chicken, more like," he said. "She's all wrinkly and funny, but Nell thinks she's beautiful."

"Mothers always do, I expect," said Jane.

"But she can't come home yet. Not till she weighs a bit more. Nell got your rosebud, by the way. She was really pleased."

"Oh good," said Jane.

"And she's called Grace – the baby, I mean. Nell said to be sure to tell you . . ."

"Oh," breathed Jane. "How lovely. It's just right . . ."

"Gosh, this was a good idea," said Tom. "You coming up the tree. Given me ideas . . ."

"Tom," Jane broke in. "Sorry. Sorry about the other day and yelling at you like that."

"You did get a bit carried away, didn't you? But I was rather asking for it. I was so excited about this place. Still I am. I went down to that mill and had a bit of a think. I mean, you were born here and it must be difficult . . . you're used to it, the same place, the same people, and being sad about the old man, and then we turn up out of the blue . . ."

"Sorry there isn't a tunnel. Really I am," Jane blurted out.

"Oh never mind that *now*," cried Tom. "Though I still think we could have a look for ourselves one day – but I've got something to show you – nothing much, but it might interest you, cheer you up . . ."

"And I've got something to show *you*," said Jane.

"Have you?" Tom sounded pleased.

"Not just to show you. Something to ask you. Something secret and mysterious – if you don't think that's too soppy a thing to say."

"Silly," said Tom. "Have you got it with you?"

"Yes, but I think it's a long job and we'll need light and pencils and paper . . ."

"Now you've got me really curious," sighed Tom. "Well, let's meet tomorrow, straight after breakfast, eh?"

"Okay, but I'd better go now," whispered Jane, disentangling her legs from the branches, twigs going off like fireworks as she slid to the ground.

"Goodnight," whispered Tom. "Oh – and – er – Jane . . ."

"What?"

"When I was down by the river – I saw it." He sounded shy in the dark.

"Saw what?"

"You *know*. The kingfisher – and – you were right. It was like catching sight of magic. Good-night."

"Goodnight, Tom."

12 . Small Greetings

As if they'd synchronised their watches on parting, Tom and Jane met in the orchard at half past eight.

"Come on," Tom said, nudging her towards the door into Mr Eliot's den.

"But the light's much better out here," said Jane. "It's a bit fiddly, you see."

"Fiddly? Oh, you mean your secret thing? But you must come in first and see what *I* . . ."

"Is there still plenty of paper in there?" Jane demanded. "And pencils?"

They tussled behind their words, each wanting to be first with the importance of their own surprise, their own secret, neither wanting to give way.

"Yes," said Tom. "On the shelf. Old score pads."

"Pencils?" Jane persisted.

"Yes," Tom sighed. "And if they're blunt I'll sharpen them with my penknife. Now come on, Jane. Please come in and have a look. It won't take long."

Tom's excitement, which so far had been crashing about all over Map's End as he made himself at home, was now fixed on something he'd done for her, specially for her. It was a very nice feeling.

"Okay, okay, okay! I'm coming," Jane laughed and gave in.

"This way." Tom bounced ahead, led Jane to her little garden, fidgeted at her shoulder as she took it all in.

"Stone the crows!" Jane cried. "Where'd you get that lovely fresh moss from?"

"Down by the mill," Tom mumbled. "And see that piece of quartz? I thought you'd like a sparkly rock."

"Oh, I do, I do. It's smashing, Tom. It's lovely. Thanks. Thanks a lot. And the pond! What have you done to the pond! It looks all new!"

"It's not new, silly. It's clean. I polished it – for hours and hours – worked all my anger at you out on that. Remember how dirty it was, all black and grimy? Well, I think it's silver. Real silver. See?" Tom turned it over, tipping its water into the moss. "It looks precious, doesn't it? And it's got a mark. Look, a shell and an initial; it's a 'P', I think. Where did you find it?"

"In the attic," Jane said anxiously. "Ages ago. I didn't think it was anything special. I just liked the shape."

"Don't worry, nobody's calling you a thief, but I think we should show it to someone some time. It's quite safe where it is for the moment."

"I wonder what it's for?" mused Jane.

"Haven't a clue," said Tom. "But it looks very old to me and sort of churchy."

Churchy. Mr Knowles's face floated through Jane's mind, then faded away like the Cheshire

Cat. "A clesi-elastical plate," she whistled softly.

"What?"

"Nothing," Jane giggled. "I'll tell you another day. Whatever it is it's very pretty. The whole garden looks very, very pretty."

"Well, will you keep it here then?" Tom urged. "Always? I wish you would. It'd only topple over in *The Ark* anyway once we get her afloat . . ."

A shiver ran through Jane. Tom was quite quite sure *The Ark* would sail again. Imagine sailing down the river, round the bend and then the next, and the next . . .

"Jane? Will you keep it here? I wish you would. You can always come in here whenever you like."

"Really?" Jane gulped. "Do you really mean it?"

"Yes," Tom said. "Nell and Dad said so. They want this to be – everybody's room."

"Well then" said Jane. "I – I think the dogs should come back and sit on the mantelpiece."

"Good idea!" said Tom. "And don't you dare start blubbing now or I'll leave immediately and I won't help you solve your puzzle – *ever*. Where is it, anyway? It had better be good!"

"Oh, it's good all right," Jane retorted.

"You don't sound too sure."

"Of course I'm sure," Jane snapped, "but . . ."

"But what?"

"I just can't make head or tail of it."

"Ja-ane, how can you know it's all right if you can't make head or tail of it?"

"Because it's from him."

"You're talking in riddles."

"It *is* a riddle. A beastly, snaky riddle."

"Why don't you just show it to me?"

"Put out your hand then." Tom obeyed and Jane dropped her mystery into his palm.

Tom hesitated. "Isn't it very private?"

"That's the trouble," Jane sighed. "It is private. Too private. Go on! Open it!"

It was Tom's turn to struggle with the bottle, fish the paper out, open it, stare at it, then turn it about clockwise, anticlockwise. He looked at Jane. "Where did you get this? Who gave it to you?"

"Mr Eliot. My friend. You know, Nell's Uncle Sam. He left it for me. I found it hidden – in one of the dogs – my dogs. They're hollow, you see. I – I – keep things in there, like he did when he was a little boy . . ."

"What sort of things?"

"Oh, sweets and feathers and – you mustn't look in there . . . ever . . ."

"Okay! Okay! I won't. Keep your hair on!"

"Anyway, once, at the beach, I told him I wished I'd find a message – in a bottle – just for me, and now he's sent me one – only look at it, Tom! Look at it! All those numbers and letters uncurling and he's even put in some *music*!"

"What fun!" Tom said happily. "I like the spiral and the mixture of clues."

"Fun?" Jane wailed. "It makes me go blank and cold."

"Fetch some pencils and paper," Tom commanded. "Of course," he boasted, "I could probably do it out of my head, but it'd take too long."

Jane hastily did as she was told, choosing to ignore, for now, the bossy Tom, the cocky Tom.

"Now!" he said. "Where to start? Let's just look at it quietly for a minute.

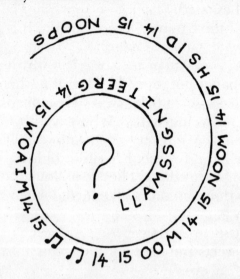

"See how the full stop in the question mark is sitting right over that 'L'? Don't you think that looks like the beginning? LLAMSSGNITEERG 1415. Llamssgniteerg! Sounds like a Welsh phone number. WOAIM 1415. Another funny phone number!" Jane leaned over his shoulder. "Don't breathe down my neck."

"Sorry, but look. The numbers are the same all the way round and there's a tiny space between the 14 and the 15. So-o-o. Go on. What's the next one?"

"14, space, 15 and then all those crotchets."

"Quavers."

"Quavers, then. What a joker!"

"Yes. He was great fun. I suppose he enjoyed doing this."

"14, space, 15," Tom mused. "Of course, in lots of codes they use the alphabet, but numbered."

"What do you mean?"

"Well, 1 stands for A, 2 equals B and so on, or, back to front, 26 is A, 25 is B and so on, down to Z which would be 1."

"Go on then!" said Jane, "hurry up and write it down and let's see what we get." She pushed past Tom, grabbed some paper and a pencil and began to dash off the alphabet in her careless, spidery writing. "One = A, two = B, three = C, four = D, 5 = E . . ."

"I'll do it backwards," Tom suggested, snatching another piece of paper. "So, 26 = A, 25 = B, 24 = C . . ."

"Sssh!" ordered Jane, her arm cradling her calculations. "You're muddling me. Don't let's say anything till we've both finished."

Tom nodded and they worked on in silence as if they were doing an exam until suddenly Jane cleared her throat impatiently. Tom looked up glumly.

"What have you got?" asked Jane.

Tom sighed. "L comes out as 15 and M as 14 and even when I turn them round to fit 14 15 it still doesn't make any sense. ML. LM. What's the difference? You look pleased with yourself. What have you got there?"

"No," smirked Jane.

"What d'you mean, 'No'?" Tom asked irritably.

"Going *forwards* 14 is N and 15 is O, so I've got No. Well, at least it's a word," Jane said smugly.

Tom looked at the spiral again. "Yes," he agreed. "And he's used the same numbers all the way round. 14 15 over and over again. LLAMSSGNITEERG NO. WOAIM NO."

Jane was peering over his shoulder again. "Look, the letters are backwards. I can see what the first word is! It's dead easy. It's S-M-A-L-L. Small. Go on, you turn SGNITEERG round! It's too long for me in my head."

Tom was already scribbling away. "G-R-E-E-T-I-N-G-S", he announced triumphantly. "Small greetings. Does that mean anything to you?"

"Mm." Jane thought for a moment. "Mm. He said something about greetings that last day at the beach . . ."

"What?" asked Tom. "What did he say?"

"He said there's a lot to be said for greetings."

"Well, that doesn't help much. Still, it's a nice way to start a message, but why *small*?"

"I don't know," Jane admitted. "And yet it makes me think of something I do know . . ."

"Let's go on," said Tom. "What comes after SMALL GREETINGS NO?"

"WOAIM."

"M-I-A-O-W," Tom announced. "Small greetings no miaow. It's daft."

"Miaow?" Jane repeated. "Cat? No cat, could it be?"

"If you say so. But what's all this?" Tom pointed

to the quavers and sighed. "NO . . . music? NO . . . song? What is he on about?"

"There's another NO coming up," warned Jane.

"NO . . . MOO," groaned Tom. "If MIAOW is cat I suppose MOO is cow . . . We'd better go on to the end and then see what it all adds up to."

"I'll read them out," said Jane. "You jot them down."

"NO . . . NOOM."

"MOON," said Tom.

"NO . . . H-S-I-D," Jane spelled out.

"Dish," said Tom.

"NO . . . NOOPS! Noops!"

"Spoon," said Tom. "Is that it, then? Is that the end?"

"Yes."

"So, what have we got? 'Small greetings, no miaow, or no cat, no music, no song, no cow, no moon . . .'"

"No dish," put in Jane. "No spoon."

"It's that old nursery rhyme! You know, 'Hey diddle diddle . . .'"

" 'The *cat* and the fiddle . . .' " Jane joined in.

" 'The *cow* jumped over the *moon*'," said Tom, jabbing at the key words.

" 'The little dog laughed to see such fun'," Jane stammered with a gulp.

" 'And the *dish* ran away with the *spoon*'," Tom finished. "But no dog," he complained. "Where's the dog, I'd like to know?"

"I *do* know," said Jane. "That's it. That's the clue. We've done it, Tom! Come on! Follow me!"

13 . The Little Dog Laughed

Now it was Jane's turn to be first, and hard for Tom to keep up with her as she shot through the orchard, tumbled over the low garden wall; hard for Tom, new to the ways of the water-meadow, to spring as surely as she did from hummock to soggy hummock, heading for *The Ark*. But he did manage, as his brains bounced about inside his skull, to work out why they were zooming in on *The Ark*. The dogs. A dog. A little dog. A little, hollow dog . . . "It's like a treasure-hunt," he puffed as he caught up with Jane, who was leaning, breathless, against *The Ark*'s gangway. "Is the next clue in one of your dogs?"

"Next clue?" groaned Jane. "I don't want any next clues. I can't do any more riddles."

"Well, whatever it is," Tom said, "it's to do with a dog."

"Of course!" Jane cheered up and began to thunder up the steps. "How close I was when I found the bottle in Large! And him lying there all the time, grinning away and me thinking he was the one who couldn't keep secrets!"

"The littlest one?" asked Tom, following her into the cabin.

"Of course. Small. Small greetings. How dumb can you be? I didn't sort that out until the very end." She stroked the little dog whose feathery tail always seemed to be very nearly wagging. "See what I mean? He's laughing. He's been laughing all this time and keeping a secret. Here . . ." she turned Middling over, rummaged around and offered Tom a fluffy, sticky fruit gum.

"Thanks," Tom mumbled. "But go on. What are you waiting for?"

"I can't bear it," Jane said. "*Not* knowing what's in there – and it might be worse, *knowing*. Ohh! I do hope it isn't another clue and we'll have to spend the rest of the holidays rushing about and tearing our brains out."

"S'all right with me," Tom slurped on his fruit gum. "But go on. Be brave. What've you got for her?" he said to Small. "Eh, little dog?"

Jane brought Small to the table, turned him upside down. "There's a thread hanging down, a little thin thread."

"Pull it!" Tom encouraged. "Pull it, then. It won't bite – not if the old man was as nice as you say he was."

Jane glared at Tom and began to pull on the thread. Suddenly with a little weighted thunk a tiny cracker landed on the table, covered in the neat writing Jane had seen before. "I knew it," she moaned. "Another clue. It's a tease, I know, a great big tease."

"No, I think it's a letter and a present," Tom said firmly, "It says there 'Dear Jane' . . ."

Jane snatched the cracker up. "Give it to me! Give it to me! Don't you know it's rude to read other people's letters?"

"Well, you won't be able to read it at all unless you undo it," Tom pointed out.

"Don't rush me," Jane begged. She shut her eyes tight for a second, opened them and very carefully eased the cracker open, like undoing a toffee you had been saving all day. All at once it was undone. In the crinkled paper nest lay a shining heap of shells. "Oh," Jane murmured. Her hand stretched over them, but she couldn't bring herself to touch them. Not just yet.

Now it was Tom's turn to breathe down her neck. "Stone the crows! Go on, Jane, pick one up. Let's see! Let's see!"

Five shells cascaded into her palm through her fingers, five silver shells, each no larger than a baby's fingertip, held together by a chain so fine and thin it looked like spider's work, the single gossamer thread of a spider's web.

"It's a necklace," she whispered.

"Shall I do it up for you?" offered Tom.

"No thanks." Jane's elbows flailed about as she struggled with the clasp. "It's minute. Lucky I've got a skinny neck. It must have been made for a very small child. But I'll wear it." Her voice quivered. "I'll wear it till it throttles me."

"Don't exaggerate," Tom said sternly.

He startled Jane. "That's what Mr Eliot was always telling me."

"Well, he wouldn't want his present to *throttle*

you, would he? Aren't you going to read his letter?"

"Of course." Jane's fingers fluttered to touch the gleaming shells as she began to read the letter out loud.

Dear Jane,
This necklace was my mother's and my
mother's mother's and so on and so forth.
I have no daughter, but I do have a friend,
a Map's End child, born and bred, who loves shells.
It was made here in New House when
New House was new. It is mine to give and now
yours to wear, or not to wear.
With love,

S. Eliot

Jane folded the letter very slowly, very neatly and put it in her pocket; she stood very still. He'd sent her a riddle and a beautiful present. But they weren't the message. Not the real message. She knew now that *that* lay inside her, waiting to fly out in a sudden, sure movement. She'd glimpse it for a second, like the kingfisher; she'd see it slip through her fingers like a moonbeam, or dazzle her like a flash of summer lightning. It would fly out of her and be passed on.

"You're not going to cry, are you?" Tom asked.

"No," Jane said. "I feel so happy I'm going to do cartwheels on the river bank."

14 . Ecclesiastical Plate

"They look as if they'd always been there," Tom stepped back to admire the dogs spaced now along the mantelpiece of the den. "Large and Middling really are a toffee-nosed pair, aren't they? But look at Small, grinning away. He looks horribly pleased with himself. You can almost see his tail wagging." Tom gave the china dog a little pat. "You were daft, you know," he said to Jane, "to think you could have kept all your things in *The Ark*. This lot would have smashed to smithereens the minute she began to run down the slipway."

Jane leaned happily into Tom's utter sureness that her boat would not be high and dry on the river bank for much longer.

"We'd better get on with *The Ark*," she said. "We haven't done any work on it for ages. Shall I help you finish the painting? Wouldn't it be great if we could launch it before it's time to go back to school?"

"Ugh!" groaned Tom. "Don't say that word! Not on a day like this! Not when the sun is baking us half to death and you've just been given a real silver necklace. But we'll have to get a move on, and there's a lot to do in the house too. I promised

Dad I'd help sort things out before Nell gets home with the baby . . ."

"Tom," said Jane. "What happened to your own mother?"

"She's dead," said Tom. "She died when I was seven."

"Do you still miss her?"

"Of course I do. Sometimes more. Sometimes less."

"I know what that's like . . . a bit. I miss Mr Eliot. I know it's not the same, but I never knew my grandfathers. He was the next best."

"It's great doing things with grandfathers," said Tom.

Friendly silence fell over the two children. Then Tom said,

"I'm sure they wouldn't want us to be sad . . . my mother, I mean, and old Sam Eliot."

And Jane felt light and free as if she had set down a heavy bag at the end of a journey and also found that someone had, unexpectedly, come to meet her. "I'll help you," she offered. "I'd really like to. Make beds and things. Clean this room out. Nell will like that rocking chair. And we could bring Stargazy down from the attic."

"Stargazy? Who on earth's Stargazy?"

"The old rocking-horse."

"You've got rockers on the brain. If you have too many rocky things in here we'll get giddy or seasick!"

"Yes, well, if you get the baby on it early enough

she'll never be a horse-hater like me," Jane pointed out.

"But she might like the fun of exploring the attic – like you did – when she's big enough," Tom suggested.

"True, perhaps it would be a pity to bring all the treasures out at once. She'll spend ages first gurgling and squawking in her pram. Then she'll start crawling everywhere and being an awful nuisance . . ."

"And staggering about on the grass out there," Tom jerked his head towards the orchard.

"Then, one day, when she's four . . ."

"Or five . . ."

"Or six . . ."

"On a rainy day . . ."

"We can take her up there and show her . . . the doll's house . . ."

"And *you* can teach her to ride!" Tom teased. "I'm starving. Do you think we could raid your mum's fridge? There's nothing to eat over here. Nell and I were supposed to go shopping yesterday but of course we . . ."

"Ssh!" said Jane. "There's someone in the kitchen!"

"That's funny." Tom lowered his voice. "Dad was going to spend all day at the hospital. Unless . . . Oh gosh! I hope everything's all right." He wheeled away to the door.

There was a cough in the passage outside the den. More footsteps, hesitant, shuffly. "Anybody at home?" an old voice quavered.

"Who can it be?" whispered Tom nervously.

"I know that voice," Jane hissed. "It's that old man."

"What old man?" Tom demanded crossly.

"It's Mr Knowles. I met him at the sale. He runs the museum in Castlebury."

"Anybody at home?" Mr Knowles sounded embarrassed; his footsteps faltered as if they would teeter out of the front door and away again if no one answered.

"Wonder what he wants." Tom opened the door. "Hullo?" he called. "We're in here. Please come in. Can I help you?"

"Ahh. Thank you. Thank you," murmured Mr Knowles. "How dark and cool it seems in the house after the merciless rays of the summer sun." His false teeth whistled merrily at every 's' they passed. "I do hope you didn't think I was an intruder . . . Well, in a manner of speaking, of course, I am, but not a criminal. Besides . . . ," he peered at Jane, still slightly sun-blind, "I believe we've met before, haven't we?"

"Yes," Jane nodded, "at the sale."

"So, you can vouch for me, so to speak. I did, in fact, knock a number of times, and then I – well, I gave the door a push, hoping there'd be somebody about at lunchtime. You see, a lid was omitted . . . hasty packing, you know. Carelessness, sheer carelessness." His teeth whistled like a kettle screaming to be taken off the boil. Jane and Tom carefully avoided each other's eyes.

"I'm sorry," Tom said. "What do you mean 'a lid was omitted'?"

"The teapots, I expect," Jane said.

"Teapots?" Tom asked.

"That's right. The teapots," Mr Knowles agreed. "The splendid teapots I acquired at the sale for my museum. A lid has been mislaid. Easily done," he whistled away, "with so small a piece. The lid consists of outsize cabbage roses . . ."

"My parents have been called away, I'm afraid," said Tom, "but please don't worry. I know nothing's been moved from the kitchen. It's probably still safely on the dresser." Tom bravely resisted the temptation to begin whistling too.

"So you're the master of the house, eh? *In loco parentis*, eh?"

"*In loco* what?"

"Taking your parents' place? Holding the fort?"

"Mrs Kingsley went to have a baby," Jane explained.

Tom frowned as if to say don't start blabbing about private things.

"A baby?" Mr Knowles repeated. "Now that is delightful, indeed delightful. Quite puts my little problem in the shade. Oh dear! I have come at a most inconvenient moment. I do apologise."

"Please don't worry," said Tom. "Why don't you sit down for a moment while I go and look for the lid and – perhaps you'd like a glass of water?"

"How kind," murmured Mr Knowles, sinking into the armchair. "How very kind. What a pleasant room," he observed to Jane when they were alone. "My eyes are becoming accustomed to its soothing light. And you, I'm sure, will enjoy the company of young Tom and his little – brother or – sister, did he say?"

"Sister," Jane said, glad Tom was not there to hear her continuing to talk about his family.

Mr Knowles smiled happily and settled himself comfortably in the chair. "Idyllic surroundings, this beautiful spot, for the childhood yearsssssss." The last 's' seemed to have been altogether too much for Mr Knowles, for all at once he sat up very straight, went very pale and began to stare at Jane in the most peculiar way. So much so that she prayed Tom would come back quickly. She wondered if she should call him, told herself not to be silly, found her hand flying to her throat.

"My dear child. I do apologise," Mr Knowles reassured her. "How careless of me. How alarming for you. I know it's rude to stare, very rude indeed. But, oh dear! Oh dear me! And I have no business to pry, to be a 'nosy parker'." The whistle began to build up once more. "But," he gulped, "how, dear child, how, may I ask, did you come by that necklace? Do you know its history?"

Confused by his excitement, his sibilant questions, his grand long sentences, Jane didn't know what to say. She was relieved when Tom came to the rescue from the doorway. "No", he said, "we don't know its history." He offered Mr Knowles a glass of water. "I'm afraid it's rather tepid. The ice thing's empty. Oh, and here's your lid."

"Ah! Safe and sound! Safe and sound! Thank you. Thank you."

"Excuse me for sounding rude," Tom continued,

"but how do *you* know the necklace *has* a history?"

"The work of Master Piers is unmistakeable," Mr Knowles announced. He sipped at his water and waited for this statement to work on Tom and Jane, but they said nothing.

"But I'm forgetting," the old man said to Jane. "You, dear child, a Map's End child no less, confessed to me, didn't you, that this name meant nothing to you? And you, my boy, are, of course, a newcomer."

"All I remember is you talked about a clesi- a clesi . . ." Jane faltered.

"Ecclesiastical plate," Mr Knowles finished for her.

"That's church silver, church gold," Jane told Tom. "You know, crosses and candlesticks . . ."

"Ah!" Mr Knowles smiled at her. "You remembered!"

"Yes, but this is a necklace!" Tom objected.

"But we have records of it! In Castlebury Museum!" Mr Knowles stabbed firmly at his armchair with a stubby finger. "Drawings, too. Unless I'm much mistaken, you, dear child, are wearing the necklace of five shells Master Piers made for his little daughter. You are not going to tell me, are you, that you found it in a Christmas cracker?"

"Heavens no!" Tom cried. "It was given to her by Mr Eliot and she's got a letter to prove it."

Jane frowned at him. Now who was blabbing?

"That makes sense! That fits! Sam Eliot was a descendant – on his mother's side, I recall." Mr Knowles began muttering to himself as if he was doing sums in his head, then nodded as if satisfied with some invisible answer.

"Would it be asking too much, Jane, to be allowed to hold it in my hand? Just for a moment? Just to look closely, briefly, at a small masterpiece?"

Tom looked fierce, prepared for action if Mr Knowles should turn into a thief and a knave before their eyes, perhaps tossing the precious trinket through the open doorway to a speedy, hidden accomplice.

But Jane heard the love and longing behind the old man's eagerness and, before Tom could stop her, had unfastened the necklace and dropped it into Mr Knowles's shaky palm. He pushed his glasses up onto his bald patch and tenderly touched the shells, turned them over, peered closely, handed the necklace back to Jane and sipped again at his water. "Oh yes," he whistled contentedly. "It is indeed the work of Master Piers. The greatest silversmith England has never known . . ."

"*Never* known?"

"Never known," Mr Knowles repeated sadly. "Never appreciated, alas! His work was too plain. No swirls. No whirls. No jewels. He was a simple man, simple in the true sense. 'A man who no more decorated his tongue with words than his chalices with frills'." Mr Knowles coughed. "But I mustn't bore you with ancient history, must I? Suffice it to say," he whistled, "the shell was his sign, and, if you look closely, you will see the initial 'P' on the back of each shell."

"P?" Tom yelped. "Shell?" He struck his forehead. "How dumb can you be? Come and look at this, then. Please, please. Quickly!" He almost dragged the astonished Mr Knowles from his chair and led him to Jane's garden.

Jane hurried after them. "Stone the crows!" she cried. "The pond. My pond." She passed it to the old man. "Look! Tom noticed it when he polished it for me. Look – a 'P' and a shell."

Mr Knowles's hand trembled. "Your pond, my dear, is a baptismal shell . . ."

"A *what*?" said Tom.

"The scoop used at christenings for sprinkling . . ."

"The water on the baby's head?" Jane interrupted. "A clesi- . . . a clesi- . . . ?" she stuttered.

"Ecclesiastical plate," Mr Knowles agreed, smiling from ear to ear. "Of the finest. Master Piers again. *Per gloriam Dei* . . ."

"*Per what*?" Tom cried.

"*Per gloriam Dei* – for the glory of God, and if I may add, for seeing it with my own eyes, *Deo gratias*."

"Day-o *what*?" Tom echoed.

"Oh, Tom, don't keep saying *what*," said Jane.

"Don't you children know *any* Latin?" Mr Knowles sounded gruff and severe, hiding perhaps his joy.

"We don't do Latin," chorused Jane and Tom.

"Don't do Latin? *Do*?" growled Mr Knowles. "Why in my day we didn't *do* Latin. We *had* Latin. Dear me! How can this be! The barbarians at the gates and yet I never met a nicer pair of young-sters."

"Sounds like mumps, having Latin!" Jane laughed.

There was an uncertain silence. Mr Knowles stroked the pretty silver shell. "I know, I know," he said at last. "Times have changed." He smiled at them both. "Old fuddy-duddy, eh? That's what comes of working in museums. You get fusty, musty. But beautiful work, isn't it? Beautiful. Treasure your necklace, Jane. Treasure it."

"Oh, I will, I will," Jane promised. "But what shall we do with the shell? Isn't it too valuable to stay in the house?"

"Perhaps," Mr Knowles suggested, "it should go into safe-keeping while I consult the Bishop of Castlebury. He might wish it to be displayed with the other cathedral treasures – for all the world to see."

"My Dad's got a safe up at the farm," said Jane. "Shall we take it to him now?"

"Good idea!" said Tom.

"Yes, indeed. Excellent," Mr Knowles whistled. "Dear me! What a day! Bless those teapots! Bless the careless mislaying of one small lid . . ." He followed them out of the front door just as Pippa came running round the corner with Alice hot on her heels like a puppy.

"Tom, Tom Piper Son!" she called.

"Ja-ane, Ja-ane," piped Alice. "Play. *Now*."

"Goodness gracious!" cried Mr Knowles, hopping skilfully out of their way.

In a rush of giddy excitement, Jane swept Alice on to her shoulders. Caught by the same feeling, Tom seized Pippa by the hand and Mr Knowles burst suddenly into song. "Here we go gathering nuts in May, nuts in May, nuts in May, on a cold and frosty morning."

All laughing at his little joke in the August sun, they set out, higgledy-piggledy and singing, for the farm.

15 . Map's End Waking

For the second time that summer Jane stood in the church, but this time not at the back, not on the edge, not with a heavy lump of iron in her throat. This time, glorying in her gossamer-fine necklace and not much minding that her mother had made her wear a dress, she stood with others in a loose circle round the font. A broad shaft of rainbow sun poured through the stained-glass windows, turning the water in the font into a dappled prism, and warming the back of Jane's legs. She looked at the baby, Grace, dozing in Nell's arms; at Robin Kingsley solemnly reading the christening service to himself; at her parents, now to become Grace's godparents, her father in his best suit, her mother in the dress she kept for weddings; at Mrs Gurney, Alice on her hip, Pippa held firmly by the hand. Tom, beside her, moved restlessly from one foot to the other. She knew why. He was waiting impatiently for this ceremony to be over so they could all get down to the real business of the day: the launching of *The Ark*.

Master Piers' shell, her pond, rested on the ledge of the font. How happy Mr Knowles had been when the Bishop had said that of course the shell must be put to its proper use whenever a child was baptised at Map's End.

The church was alive with relaxed sounds. The mothers murmured over Grace's head. The vicar's cassock rustled and swished as he joined them at the font. Pippa swung on Mrs Gurney's hand and crooned some small song. Alice sucked her thumb wetly as if it was the most delicious lollipop in the world. Tom dropped his prayer book. Laughter floated just above them all and in the black belfry Scully Jenkin and his bell-ringers shuffled and coughed. They had rung the christening party in with a boisterous peal which had sounded to Jane just like 'Upon Paul's steeple stands a tree'. Now they were waiting to ring them out again. It had been Mrs Gurney's idea that there should be bells, that Grace should be welcomed 'extra loud', as she put it, since she'd had such a difficult start.

"Pretty," said Alice, making a sudden dart and grab at Jane's necklace.

"I want to see the wa-a-a-ter," Pippa whined, climbing onto the steps on the font on tiptoe. "I want to see the w-a-a-a-ter."

"Now sssh the both of you," whispered Mrs Gurney. "Ssh."

" 'Dearly beloved'," said the vicar, rather suddenly. " 'Parents and godparents, we are here this afternoon to welcome . . .' "

Dreamily Jane let the first words wash over her. I'll need a new pond, she said to herself. A shallow shell will do. I could paint on that . . . paint a starfish . . . silver . . . or gold . . . Then Tom

prodded her with his elbow, pointing to the open prayer book he had been sharing limply with his father.

" '. . . everlasting God,' " the vicar was praying. Tom pointed, picking out the bits of the prayer he liked as if they were the cherries in a dull cake. " 'God . . . who didst save Noah and his family *in the Ark* . . . look upon this child that she may be *received into the ark* . . . of . . . the church . . .' "

"She will be," Tom muttered to Jane, head well down. "She will be. In about half an hour." He smiled at Jane, and Robin Kingsley shook his head mildly at them both.

Tom tried to stand still. Jane tried to listen to the words, but she was really only waiting to see how the shell was used and wondering if Grace would mind being sprinkled with cold water, and looking forward to the party they were going to have on the water, in *The Ark*. But she did understand that her own parents had promised now to be Grace's godparents. She did understand that Grace was being welcomed. She wondered why she didn't remember being a baby, wondered if *any*one remembered being a baby.

Then, at last, the vicar gently took the baby in his arms and the silver shell flashed in the sun's great rays as he plunged it into the water and sprinkled a few drops onto the baby's forehead. Grace began to yell.

"Cry baby," said Pippa, hopping on and off the steps of the font.

"Get down," said Mrs Gurney.

"Baby crying," said Alice. Mrs Gurney shook her gently, laid a finger over her lips. "Ssh, now, ssh."

Grace yelled and yelled. She yelled through the Lord's Prayer; she yelled through the Blessing. Pippa and Alice fell silent, still, smug. And then the bells began to peal. Everyone turned anxiously towards the crimson, hiccupping Grace.

"Oh dear," Mrs Gurney sighed. "Perhaps she didn't need an extra loud welcome after all." But as the bells grew louder, Grace's kitten-like sobs grew weaker and weaker. Her eyelids began to close, the crotchety puckers faded from her face and she fell fast asleep, tightly safe in the crook of Nell's arm.

Jane was longing to get down to *The Ark* to help Tom and his father, Scully and his bell-ringers put the planks into place for the launch, but her mother caught her at the kitchen door. "Don't go emptyhanded," she said. "Here, darling, take this basket down to where Nell is sitting with Grace and I'll be along in a minute with the cake."

"Funniest ice-bucket I ever saw," laughed Mr Finch as he emptied ice cubes into a battered milking pail. "I'm not bringing the champagne out till the very last minute, so get a move on you two! I don't want to miss all the fun."

"All right! All right! Don't fluster me," Mrs Finch cried. "Oh dear, we've forgotten the glasses."

Jane left her parents arguing amiably and hurried down to Nell sitting on the river bank in the shade of the willows. Grace stirred softly in her lap.

"What fun," said Nell. "A christening party on the water."

"I hope it doesn't sink or anything!" Jane worried.

"What?! After all the work you and Tom, not to speak of the dads, have put into that hull? I'm sure if you wanted you could rename it *The Unsinkable*!"

"What does it feel like when the baby kicks?" Jane asked. "When it's still inside you, I mean."

Nell drew up Grace's lacy christening dress. "Put your hand against her feet," she said. The waking baby yawned and stretched as Jane's giant hand spanned her warm, silky soles and ten wriggling toes. "It feels like . . . like a cat's paw pushing into your cheek," Jane decided.

"That's a good way of putting it," Nell agreed.

"Oh good," Jane said. "Here come Mum and Dad, at last!" In procession along the farm side of the river bank her mother led the way to *The Ark*, holding high a huge cake, while her father followed slowly, carefully with his glassy, icy cargo.

The figures scurrying around *The Ark* looked like busy insects at work on a fallen tree; and from behind Jane came the wood-pigeon voice of Mrs Gurney, the skylark piping of the little girls.

"Teatime! Teatime!" Pippa called.

"Where's the teatime?" Alice demanded.

"On the boat," puffed Mrs Gurney. "We're going to have tea on the boat. Now come and sit down a minute, you two." She lowered herself to the ground. Pippa leaned against her and Alice tumbled like a puppy into Jane's lap.

"This heat," Mrs Gurney sighed. "I never thought I'd wish for a cooling drop of rain."

"Poor Mrs Gurney," said Nell, "and you've been run off your feet for days . . ."

"And nights," Mrs Gurney grinned. "But never mind. Their mum and dad'll be over tomorrow to fetch them home. Then I can put my feet up good and proper." She stretched her legs out in front of her and wiggled her feet. "Still, it's been a lovely day, a lovely summer. Everything's turned out well, hasn't it? You've got your lovely baby, a lovely new home. These little 'uns have had all the fresh air and more. Harvest looks good. Jane's had a lovely present from a dear old friend – and found herself a nice new friend. Oh yes, all very satisfactory."

"But what about Mr Gurney?" Jane asked, aghast suddenly at the thought of him, always on his own, pacing the downs.

"What about Mr Gurney, dear?"

"He hasn't found his orchid."

"Ooh, don't you worry about him, my dear. I don't think he'd like it one little bit if he *did* find it! Then what'd he do? I think he prefers his looking to his finding. Oh no, Jane, don't trouble your head over my old man."

"Ja-ane!" called Tom. "What d'you think you're doing lolling about in the shade? Come and lend a hand."

At Tom's shout a heron rose, soaring then

sinking again to some quieter, more distant pool.

"Coming!" cried Jane. "Coming!" She sprang up and began to leap the short-cut way across the soggy water-meadow.

"Shoulder to the pump!" shouted Mr Finch. "One, two, three, *heave*!"

"One, two, three, *heave*!" Scully and his men took up the song.

One shove, a second shove, a third almighty shove, and *The Ark* began to slither and jerk down the home-made slipway, and all of a sudden, with a huge splash, she was afloat. Mr Kingsley and Mr Finch moored her safely, looking as if they had been at sea all their lives.

"Hooray!" cried Tom.

"Hooray, hooray!" Jane joined in and began to clap her hands.

And then, the message came. Like a blue glimpse of the kingfisher's wing, like the uncatchable moonbeam, like a flash of summer lightning. Jane heard Mr Eliot's voice inside her, or as if he were there, near, just behind her. *Join in, join in.* And she began to run. She never felt her flying feet touch the ground. She flung herself on her knees in front of Nell, undid the necklace, held it out. "Here. Please. This is for Grace. I want it to be for Grace. Mr Eliot said 'to wear, or not to wear.' Grace is the newest. I don't need it any more." And she turned and ran, ran back to Tom, to her father, to her mother, to *The Ark* and the wide, wide river.